YAAKOV C LUI–HYDEN

Jael: The Lord's Archer

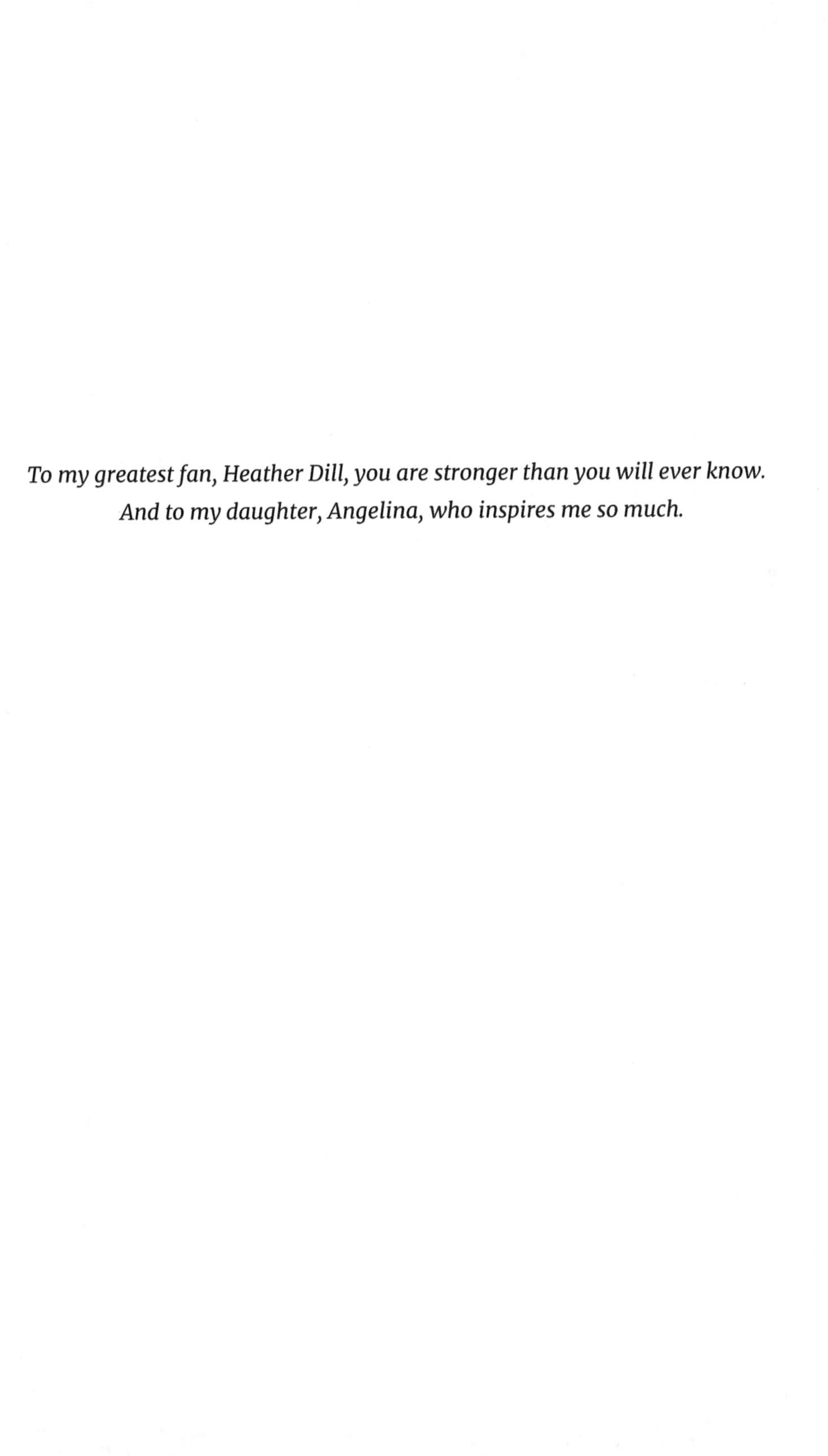

*To my greatest fan, Heather Dill, you are stronger than you will ever know.
And to my daughter, Angelina, who inspires me so much.*

Contents

Prologue

It was hard to know if the pungent smell came from the walls or his own vomit. It had been at least three days, wandering aimlessly surrounded by wet moss, stone and his feet kicking up against rat ribs.

The string Ariadne had given him had disappeared from his hand. He didn't even know when it had escaped him.

His torch flame had extinguished after a few hours and he was left alone in the dark, unsure of the way forward and with little prospect of finding the way back.

His eyes never truly adjusted to the gloom, though some of the moss seemed to glow a pale green, throbbing randomly with colour.

There had been a few missing bricks at first, bringing in shafts of light, but no longer. As he descended, and it was clear he was descending, the air grew warm, oppressive and stale.

And then there was the smell of decay, the smell of defeat of all those who had come before. Now here he was, a fool who might as well be blind.

All this, for promises of love, glory and a waiting father back home.

He still had his dirk in his belt, his only comfort, but against the beast his prospects were dim as his surroundings.

But Theseus always felt the luck of the gods – that they had their eye on him and gave their protection. He would sacrifice an animal if he got back, no, when he got back.

Now, though, the time was urgent. He was weak from the vomiting, the ripe smell was half seaweed and half maggot infested corpse. He could not will his stomach into complying and acid burned at his already dry throat.

The air failed to move, and each step was heavy, as he was wracked with coughs and delirium called him like a Siren.

One foot in front of the other, he trudged forward, sandals crackling on soft bones underfoot.

There! He heard it and grimaced, He moved to his left and found the wet, slimy wall and froze.

That noise, that roar, echoing through the dark. The roar of the Minotaur.

***

It had been two days since he had heard the beast. A week down here, with no sustenance and a few days since he had tried the putrid water that dripped down the walls.

The beast would not have to kill him; he would die in this maze from thirst or hunger before then.

To make matters worse, his dirk had slipped off in the darkness, and scurrying around on his knees for some hours found nothing. Now he held a bone as a weapon, human or animal he knew not.

***

Love had been left behind in the Palace. His life before drained away into the ever dark. Hour by hour the humid air sapped his strength, sucked out the marrow of his bones until he was a husk. Less man that the Minotaur he hunted.

Yet in the dark, yet in the solitude, some semblance of humanity remained. Though all he wielded was a sharp bit of bone, he was Theseus and had the fire of man within him.

"I must go on; the Minotaur might consume my flesh, but he'd have to fight for every morsel."

A slight movement of air told him that another passage went off to his left. Until now, his purpose had been true, and he had hugged the right wall, but he was no closer to his prize. And perhaps his time was short. He turned and found the walls of the passage and took a step into it.

It was then, the surrounding walls brightened and he could see all the stonework, every crack, every bit of moss and on the floor skeletons of those who have been before.

Puzzled, he looked around for the source of the light, which was getting stronger and stronger until he realised it was coming from behind. From the passage he had just left.

Stepping back the way he came, as the Sun burns bright, so the passage was illuminated. Such intensity scorched his eyes, and he fell back screaming as if hot metal was poured between his eyelids.

He staggered as blood and tears poured down his face.

But he had seen what he had seen within the blaze. A powerful man with the face of a lion marching with spear in hand, giant wings on his back.

Whatever it was, it was no Minotaur. And in his life of service to the gods he had never felt such power, such presence. Somehow he knew this creature was not for him, but was hunting the Minotaur too.

***

Eyes bleeding in the dark. A whimpering, broken man. He could not open his eyes any longer as he sat down, leaning against the cold stone work and knowing death would come for him soon. What had he seen? What manner of creature was it? Such power, such majesty.

Time went by until he felt something, felt a warmth, and affection here in the cold maze. Felt something there, another presence. Like the one before but softer, gentler and light throbbed up against his sore eyes.

His eyes opened to the light, and a blurred image of the woman towered over him.

"Forgive Raphael, he has recently been in the throne room of the Most High. It is difficult for mortals to gaze upon his countenance."

This made no sense at all.

"Here." He felt the woman kneel and her hand covered his eyes and she said something under her breath in a language he didn't understand.

Warmth, life, love. His spirit field with rigour and vitality. The fog over his eyes lifted and the woman, the beautiful tall woman with golden hair, came into focus. The power coming from her, surely she was also one of the gods?

"Better?"

He nodded and glanced down at his hands and stood. Every bone, every muscle coursed with energy, like age being defeated.

"Who are you?"

"I am Shaerlyn. I am a servant of the Most High God."

"Zeus?"

"No, child. Come." She took his hand "We are to rid this labyrinth of its beast."

Then she turned and walked back towards the tunnel where she came, her height easily double his.

With little hesitation, Theseus scurried after her and stayed within her light.

***

Something was happening, something was changing. Being near this tall woman had his memories flood back. The five challenges on the road to Athens, the defeat of the Marathonian Bull. A task only achieved by one other, Hercules years earlier. So the story was told. He thought about his father and finally being recognized as his son and heir.

And the demands of the King of Crete -14 Athenians to be sacrificed to the Minotaur. All for the tragic slaying of his son.

Theseus promised his own father to slay the beast instead.

Now he was here in the labyrinth with his love, Ariadne, awaiting him above. She had given him the string to find his way back, the string now lost in the dark.

He was not alone, though; he was with this tall woman who strove with purpose. Who was she? And who was her companion who stalked the other tunnel? Gods? Titans? Or something else?

All he knew was walking behind her and watching the glorious sway of her hips. He had all the power and strength he previously possessed, perhaps more. And a sense of peace, of belonging, of kindness. Something else... This woman had determination.

The woman stopped abruptly and seemed to be listening. Moments passed, then she pulled out a giant flaming sword. Her green eyes swung down at him "The battle is joined ahead. We must hurry!"

Theseus nodded, but before he could say anything, the woman was charging away down the tunnel. He leapt after her, to stay always in her light, yet he carried no weapon for battle.

They rushed into a large chamber and were alerted to the clash of steel as the brightly lit and lion-faced companion fought off the Minotaur with the spear. The Minotaur, far more fierce than any of Theseus' dreams, parried away the spear with a giant axe, a whip in his other hand.

Theseus looked at the ground and saw it littered with bones, swords, spears and shields. Instinctively he grabbed a shield and spear and poised himself to attack, just as the woman stepped forward as well.

From the depths of the chamber, still shrouded in shadow despite the pair of beings of light, came a hoarse laugh and then the ground shook as a new beast step forward. Another Minotaur, a much larger one with blue matted hair and green glowing eyes.

"Asterion." The woman breathed. Theseus looked from the woman to the beast in wonder.

The beast spoke "I no longer go by that name. For now, I am Baal. Worshipped by many. And here... Making quick work of... Raphael, I believe? Is my son, Hai Chen. You are outmatched angel and today you will fall. Both of you will fall and serve me and I will consume your pet human friend."

"None pass the sword." The woman said and stepped in front of Theseus to shield him. But Theseus was a warrior, a veteran of battle, and he needed no such protection.

The blue-skin Minotaur stepped forward, he was at least five times the girth of the woman, but with flaming sword in hand she did not seem to fear him.

There was a clash of metal to their right and Theseus turned as the lion-faced creature pushed the smaller Minotaur back onto a series of steps. The Minotaur responded by lowering its head and charging, driving a sharp horn into its foe.

"Raphael!"

The woman charged across the room to intervene, but the blue giant Minotaur stepped forward and swatted her away.

Theseus reacted and sprung forward and launched his spear into the giant beast's side. The creature merely snorted and looked at him and then stepped further towards the woman.

Theseus studied the floor and saw another spear, grabbed it and threw it. Again, no reaction. The woman was clambering to her feet with the sword in front of her as the beast seemed to laugh.

The Athenian grabbed a short sword and ran at the creature who would pay for ignoring him. Just as the Minotaur reached the woman, Theseus ran up the beast's arm and hurled himself at its face, sword true–blade sliding into its eye.

That got a response, and the beast howled as he landed underneath it and drove his sword again and again into its hide.

A giant fist smash into his shield and he was launched backwards, slamming into the wall with the wind taken out of him.

But it worked. The beast distracted, missed parrying the flaming blade that sliced down into its shoulder and then swung up and took off the Minotaur's head.

The woman stood over the beast for just a moment and pulled out some chain and tied it around one of the creature's arms.

And then, for a moment, a feeling of dread, a feeling of every rotting and decaying thing, of worms crawling over his bones. A man appeared like the

Charon that guard the river Styx. And this man took the chain and with giant wings flew up through the rock and was gone. Taking the giant Minotaur with him.

The smaller Minotaur was now in a panic, as the woman and lion- faced man surrounded him.

"Time for you to join him," Said the lion man.

The Minotaur scanned the room for escape, but there was none.

Then his eyes settled on Theseus, crumpled in the corner and the beast seemed to smile and in a moment lower its head and charged.

Theseus' sword had been knocked away, but he still had his shield and he sucked in air as he tried to raise it to have any chance of absorbing the blow..

"He's going for the soulgate!" He heard the woman shout.

The fierce eyes were upon him, the face in a snarl. He raised his shield and closed his eyes for the bone crushing doom.

Then, silence.

The woman sighed and walked over to him and pulled him up. The lion- face approached also, and he realized he could now withstand the glare.

"What happened?" Asked Theseus.

"The Minotaurs are gone." The woman smiled at him "And it's time for us to go too. You fought well, Theseus, and Athens awaits you to rejoice. Follow that passage and do not deviate, I will light torches before you. At the end you will find another antechamber and turn left to walk across it. There you will find the string that led you into the maze. But note, though you have love in your heart, you have much work to do in Athens and this is no place for Ariadne, daughter of King Minos. You have a difficult choice to make, but the choice is yours. Farewell, our work is done."

With that, wings exploded from their backs and the two soared through the tunnels, lighting the way as they left. Theseus stood in the last great home of the Minotaur, one man living among so many slain. He took a spear in hand, his shield in the other, and began his journey back through the labyrinth. Unsure how they knew of him, his life, and why they had saved him.

1

Chapter 1

L earning to ride is quite a challenge. My bicycle still has training wheels, and it is clear I still need them. Sometimes I forget about the brakes and just run into things! My mother says I am a bit clumsy, but I will grow out of it.

We don't do a lot of rabbit shooting any more and never go away again hunting. Just once a week, my father goes and it is still rabbit stew most nights. We have a boat now in the backyard on a trailer, but we haven't used it yet. My greatest possession though is my bike.

I ride all the time, morning to night. Soon it would be time to go to school, I am going to start earlier than other children because my birthday is in July and the school year is from January. So I can start half a year early or half a year later.

My sisters have been going to school for ages, I am not so sure about the experience. Mum tells me it is an opportunity to meet new friends and other kids to play with, but I have plenty of friends already. I often miss my sisters during the day, they are away so long. I don't think I could be away from my mother as much as they are.

I become braver on the bike and even go around the block. It feels strange not to be on my street. James Blundie has a bike too, and sometimes we ride together.

We often have races down the street, which I always win, but sometimes I crash when I forget about the brakes or press the wrong one.

It is okay, though, I run to Mummy, and she fixes everything. My bike never breaks no matter how many times I crash it.

We are over the Driscoll's place all the time now. Dad never asks me to come shooting on Sundays, so I go to Church and Sunday School. Church is sooooo boring! I am lucky if I don't fall asleep. They have nice sweets and cakes afterwards, and Sunday school is okay because we sing a lot of songs. Afterwards, we normally go for lunch at the Driscoll's or occasionally they come to our place. It is usually theirs, though.

This I always prefer because of the toys. Despite my sisters being friends with the two girls, I am always the one who wants to go over there to play. They also have lots of board games like snakes and ladders and we play a card game called Uno. I could understand this one, but other card games are too hard for me.

***

I admit I am nervous, and that is a new feeling for me. Now I know about the butterflies in the stomach. James Blundie isn't going to school till next year so I will know NOBODY!

My sisters don't even go to the same school as me; they go to a bigger school. I do look very smart in my blue uniform, though. Dad says I am a 'heartbreaker' and a 'ladykiller'.

I share my room now at the back of the house with my baby brother, Stuart. He is sooo fat! He is already walking but prefers just to lie around. Sometimes I even feed him in the high chair.

He doesn't play much though, mostly sleep and keep to himself. He is talking, but he won't run around like I do.

I play with him a lot though, and I wonder if he will miss me when I am at school. I am a big boy now.

Mum took a photo of me in the yard and said she is very proud of how I looked for school. My hair doesn't not always stay down and she spits on her hand and pats it down, I don't like that much.

***

The school isn't far, and I have walked much, much further but for the first day Mum is going to take me in the car.

The school has lots of pretty paintings on the outside, even one of Mickey Mouse. It is quiet as everyone is inside as we are late. I worry I will forget to go to the toilet; I seem to have a problem with this. Mum explains that if I need to go to the toilet, I should raise my hand and ask the teacher, but I am shy.

Mum has packed me two sandwiches for lunch, a banana and an apple. I don't really like apples, but Mum says they are good for my teeth. Still, I much prefer oranges and bananas. Everyone else seems to prefer apples. Maybe I can swap with someone at lunch?

Mum takes me to an old lady behind a desk and she speaks encouragingly to me while my mother filled in some forms. Mum explains she will meet me right here after school.

She kissesme, and then the old lady takes my hand and leads me to the class.

***

Ok so the first day wasn't so bad. We played this game throwing a ball to each other, and I had some trouble with it, but I met some nice kids. There was this girl called Amy who lived on my street and a couple of other kids who had their dads in the Navy too. They gave me some street names, but I would have to ask my Mum where they were.

I had no accidents at school today; I made sure I went to the toilet at recess and lunch like Mum had suggested as well.

There she is. The most beautiful person in the whole wide world, arms outstretched for me to run into. I charge down the little path and give Mum the biggest of big, big hugs.

She asks me about my day, and I tell her everything. I ask about the street names and one was behind our street. I will ride my bike there one day after school and see if I can see Peter's house. He hasn't told me the number, but maybe he will be playing outside?

The trip home is quick. Mum tells me we will walk to school tomorrow.

I get home and run to my room to find my baby brother. He is asleep! I put my bag down quietly and look at him. He is too big to carry now. He has blonde hair and blue eyes. Eyes like my dad, like I wanted.

I go to the lounge room as Mum gets me some biscuits and milk. I have some new Lego, and I consider playing with that, but I think it is better to see James Blundie and then ride to Peter's if I have time.

In moments, I am on my bike, peddling away furiously.

***

I still worry about the toilet, as sometimes the classes are too long. Sometimes I have accidents, and this is very embarrassing. You can't say it wasn't me when your pants are wet!

One thing I notice is girls always smelt prettier than boys. Sometimes the boys would fart and everyone would laugh or giggle, but I never heard the girls do this. I wonder even if they can. Was it just boys who farted?

I am doing okay at school, but I am much smaller than everyone else and also not good at the ball games at all. What I am good at are games that involve a lot of running or hiding. I once hid outside the school gates, but if a teacher caught me, I would have been in big trouble.

I find Peter's house on my third attempt and we hang out together. I introduce him to James Blundie but, although we played well in the sandpit with James' Tonka trucks, I don't think Peter liked James that much.

I would always like anyone who had the same name as Dad and I!

***

Shaerlyn had taken her time to rest, but still monitored even those who watched over young James. The soulgate remained unchanged on Asgrax, so she was blessed now with Nephis and Farida of her kinfolk. These two took her place for a time as guardians of the boy, but also gave her fellowship and company. From her cave, they could take turns to travel down and view James.

Farida was no warrior. She was a singer of one of the highest voices. She had been known as the beacon, as she stood so close to the throne she always shone, and her voice could travel through space and spirit with ease, such was its majestic power.

Nephis, Shaerlyn had known for a long while, and their paths had crossed more than once. Nephis was a warrior, donned head to toe in Bronze armour. He was cherubim, like Shaerlyn, far less common than the usual archon soldier.

He was strong of build, normally 12 feet in height, his skin matching his armour's colour. He was most known for his indiscretion at the battle of Troy, when he was forced to draw arms on a demonic horde and reveal himself. Stories abound of his exploits on the battlefield that day, most of them now just myth and legend. Chastised later, on the day, his appearance had led to victory for those inspired by his presence.

After that, he faded from view, called in once to defend Rome at a time the church was in its infancy. He then went east into the Byzantine and became the city guardian of Constantinople for what it seemed was a millennium.

He re-emerged in the era of the Crusades, where the hearts of men were in fervour but often misplaced. Such destruction, such heresy and such loss of life occurred in this time. Noble knight became a savage, a savage showed nobility. There were lights that shone in this darkness, but so many were drowned out even by their very own. The people lost their way and superstitions took hold. The armies of Evil launched attack on attack and proved even bolder than they had before. Archons marched out of Heaven in their thousands, some to never return. Nephis was made a General and rallied the troops in defiance of the increasing armada trying to encircle them. Nephis won an epic battle, when even Michael had been put in danger, and thus Nephis retired into the post of defense of Heaven itself. Fit reward for one who had done so much.

To have both he and Farida here, Shaerlyn could actually rest. Perhaps if others had been so chosen by her King she would have worried some. Her King always knew best and rewarded those who displayed such trust and loyalty. She should never doubt HIS wisdom, no matter who HE sent.

Farida's sweet voice had driven the forgotten ones to the far ends of the planet. Her voice was like the tree of life or the river. It filled Shaerlyn to overflowing and the walls of the cave sang long after she had finished. Destined to sing, the King had sent her as muse to sing prophecies, visions and dreams into a young David's head. Such a more famous psalm never existed than the one she helped inspire David to write during a time when David was in doubt and in pain.

Jael visited too from time to time, but he had a new mission elsewhere. A new decade had begun on Earth, and things were constantly changing. Just in the last year, Pol Pot was overthrown, as was Idi Amin, which had been a relief to many. Saddam Hussein and Margaret Thatcher became leaders of their respective countries. Iran became an Islamic republic and the Shah was no more, Russian troops took control of Afghanistan and a man known as the Unabomber struck terror into the hearts of the American people.

It seems things were getting clearly more difficult and Shaerlyn hoped that this new decade would be a more peaceful one than the one before. When she looked on young James, something her kinfolk resisted her doing for now, she saw his eyes bright and full of hope. In his world, every day was a time for laughter and fun, although he was getting into the habit of pranking rather too easily. He had already had the Mumps, and no doubt other sicknesses would come across him. Despite his mother's religious grooming of his hair and frequent washing, Shaerlyn spotted the eggs that would soon make his scalp itchy and probably limit his time at school. His friend Peter clearly had lice already and was probably the carrier. Young James didn't really take to pain so well as some. She wished she could comfort him in the same ways of old, but it was impossible now. James would never remember her.

***

It was very exciting, for a special treat, Dad said we would go to the cinema where they have a big screen and popcorn. I have always wanted to try popcorn.

Anne and Margaret were fighting over the seats in the car as always, Stuart was just sitting in the back seat, not seeming to care what was going on. It was a tight fit with my sisters fighting, but Dad wouldn't let me climb over the back to the back seats. I liked them; they faced behind us not in front and I could play with my toys there. But I would often get car sick back there, besides there were all kinds of things Dad had in the back. So I will just have to put up with my sister's elbows.

My town didn't have a cinema, so we would drive to Frankston. Mum worried we would be too late and not be able to buy Popcorn.

***

Shaerlyn smiled as the family fought their way into the car and drove away. Her double pair of wings broke out from her back and she took to the evening sky. She wouldn't be able to eat popcorn, but she was curious about this cinema experience. She decided it was worth seeing and headed to Frankston above the Campbell's car.

***

I have just seen an amazing film. 'The Empire strikes back.' Oh, it was so good! Apparently it is the second movie and my parents have promised me I can watch the first movie when it comes out on TV.

It starts off on a snow planet and there is this evil man named Darth Vader, who is hunting down the people called the rebels. Darth Vader is soooo cool! I wasn't afraid of him, unlike my brother, but I could just feel how powerful and awesome he was.

The stormtroopers in the movie are really cool too, and when I grow up, I want to be something like them. This movie really has captured my imagination. I started building space ships out of Lego, but what I really want are the toys. I beg and beg to get some of the action figures. I saw one called Boba Fett and I like him the best. I also found out I hate popcorn, I mean really hate it. Even the smell. But my sisters wouldn't stop eating it in the cinema, and I was glad to be home. If the cinema meant that smell, I think I would stay home next time. I think I am old enough now to stay home by myself.

2

Chapter 2

The seagulls squawked and circled around her feet as she dropped bread to them.

She gazed over the water to the rest of the city on the other side. Today the wind was up and the Bosporus had small choppy waves that danced against the rock wall harmlessly.

That wonderful fresh sea air. Ferries navigating larger ships, tiny fishing boats littering all space in-between. It was a hive of activity and lifeblood to the city.

Ruzanna strolled on, leaving the birds to fight for the crumbs. Behind her, two Janissary walked in silence, her eternal guardians.

She gave them no thought. Her graceful strides caused traffic chaos and cyclists and scooter riders crashed into the roadside or had to even be fished out of the water. She always had this effect on men, which just showed how disciplined her guards must be.

She liked this part of the city, with classical homes that were former Ottoman estates and homes for the privileged. There was far less activity on the roadside than on the water, how the waterway was crowded!

It was a little after noon when she heard the flutter of wings which belonged to no bird; she turned and her face lit up.

"Jael, could it be that you miss me?"

The archon stood before her but invisible to all but her.

"Well, we were having a conversation last time and I don't like to keep things unfinished."

Ruzanna offered the crock of her arm, and Jael slid his hand in and walked beside her. It might have been a peculiar look to see her walking so, but people would hardly be focused on that.

Just her walking, arm in arm, with the invisible.

A perfect day in Istanbul.

***

Oh, I just saw the first Star Wars, the real Star Wars! It was on television last night. Perfect timing! This movie starts on a desert world. I think I am in love with Princess Leia.

I couldn't help myself. And my annoying sister Margaret has to make fun of me about it too.

I hope I get some Star Wars toys for my birthday or Santa brings me some. I have been a good boy.

***

I was too young for my first Olympics and don't remember them at all but in 1980, around the time of my birthday, it was the summer Olympics in Moscow!

Dad told me that the Soviets had done something bad in Afghanistan and that meant absolutely nothing to me at all. All I know was Dad almost went to the Olympics, he could have if he tried, and now he trained many Olympic athletes. Maybe he wasn't going to get a gold medal at the Olympics, but I know I will. One day, when I'm bigger.

Because the Soviets had done this bad thing, Australia couldn't march into the stadium with the Australian flag. This was important to Dad, but I didn't understand why. I just like the big giant torch and teddy bear.

There was a song that all of us would sing "Moscow, Moscow, have you seen my teddy bear, marching in its underwear aha ha ha ha hey!" I was told these were not the real words to the song but I think our words were better.

Dad explained a lot of the sports to me. He was particularly interested in the 1500 m between Sebastian Coe and Steve Ovett. He couldn't decide who would win but said that maybe I would run this distance one day and the 800 m. But I was only interested in the 100 m, the 200 m and the long jump looked cool too. Oh, and the pole vault.

The cycling was interesting too, and Dad made a big fuss about Kenrick Tucker, an Australian from Rockhampton. Dad was born in Mount Morgan just outside Rockhampton and grew up there, so he was excited to see a local boy compete at the Olympics. He watched every competition and Dad said Kenrick Tucker had legs like tree trunks. He said his legs were so big because he was a sprinter, but Dad was a sprinter and didn't have legs like Kenrick Tucker.

One of Dad's favourite sports was the Decathlon, and there was a man from Great Britain called Daley Thompson. Dad explained he was so gifted in all the power sports that all he had to do is finish the 1500 m event to win. This was his hardest event for him, but he only had to finish it.

I turned five, but it was a small celebration because last year I got my bicycle and I don't think my parents had much money. It was okay, I would wait for Santa at Christmas. No Star Wars toys, but I think Santa will listen to me. I even wrote them on a list which I gave Mum and she said she would make sure Santa would get it. Mum knew everyone!

After my birthday, there was only one event my father was interested in, it was the Marathon. Dad told me he worked alongside Robert de Castella, a marathon runner, and Robert de Castella was in the Olympics. Dad didn't think he could win but told me stories about how Robert would train doing 40 400 m runs in a row in less than one minute each with a jog recovery between each run. Dad said that was amazing, I have no idea.

The Olympics closed, and all we were left with was that Moscow song. And, for me, the determination that I would be an Olympic champion too one day.

***

I couldn't believe it. One day at teatime Dad announced we were moving. And not just down the road, either. To a new State, New South Wales, and I would go to a new school.

I wasn't happy at all. James Blundie wouldn't be coming with us or Peter or Amy or any of my friends. I wouldn't be able to see the Driscolls or play with their toys. Dad promised we could come back and visit and that we could probably still find rabbits to hunt. By now, I was quite an excellent shot with the rifle, but I never fired the pistol again.

After dinner, I went to my room and cried. I don't know why I was crying so much. Also, the boat in the backyard was to be sold and I would miss the Orange tree there too. My world was changing, Anne and Margaret were excited. Stuart couldn't care less, all he was interested in was eating. But I had friends and my room. I didn't understand why we had to move at all.

***

"Excuse me, young lady. Is this seat taken?"

Shaerlyn whirled in confusion. "You can see me?"

"Of course. Now, is this seat taken?"

Shaerlyn's eyes widened at the old bent-over man, leaning on a cane in one hand, and the other nursing a box of popcorn.

"Perhaps I will sit somewhere else?" The man said and began to trot away.

"No, please stay." Shaerlyn said. If only to get some answers…

The man seemed satisfied and sat down next to her. "So, are you excited about the movie? I hope it is good as the first one."

"I… Never saw the first one, but I heard about it."

"Interesting choice of names, don't you think? I mean… Kal–EL. Is he supposed to be a relation of yours?"

"I don't understand."

"Well, of El is often used for angels, no? And since you are one…"

"Sorry? Could you repeat that, I think I misheard."

"Relax, Shaerlynel. I am just toying with you."

"Who are you!"

"Shhhh shhhh." Whispered a woman in the row in front.

Shaerlyn lowered her voice. "Who are you?" Her eyes narrowed. "Reveal yourself in HIS name!"

The face changed, and she saw her dear brother, Jael, next to her. Grinning broadly.

Shaerlyn swung her arm up and punched him in the nose. "I can't believe you did that to me. Why are you as a human?"

"How else am I going to enjoy popcorn?"

There was a hush sound again from the row in front.

Jael said, "Let's take this to a quieter place, shall we? Nether or Ethereal plane?"

Shaerlyn raised an eyebrow. "Well, not Nether. We wouldn't see much of the movie. Let's go to the Ethereal plane."

"Agreed." Jael said.

The world around them took a pinkish red hue, crackling with electricity. Shaerlyn rarely ventured into the Ethereal plane, the physical world was like a mask over what was here. Honesty, raw energy. She surveyed the room and saw the interaction of every atom, every cell, every light fitting, the projector, and every beating heart and every neuron firing. Some on Earth, she knew could glimpse upon this plane; she didn't understand how or why. Hear and see electricity radiating off objects, something that could overwhelm the mind.

She looked over to James who was lit up with such potential then she casually turned her gaze towards his mother and gasped.

"The mother, I didn't know."

"Oh? How long have you been taking care of this boy? You have spent no time in the Ethereal plane?"

"Well, no threat ever comes from the Ethereal plane, so I paid no heed. I did not know, I really did not know."

Jael chuckled, "You've just been using the Ethereal plane to throw your weight around?"

"Yes! I move my mass in here, for speed, bring it in and out. But when I'm doing that, I don't have time to admire the view."

"Well, fair enough."

"Does she know? Can she know?"

"I hardly think so."

"She is blessed! That's why I haven't been able to see her angel. I don't even know if she has an angel. If she needs one?"

"The Lord works in mysterious ways, Shaerlynel. Although such blessed are often recalled so soon. Their lives are usually challenging, transforming, impacting the souls of others. But it's a hard path, but with the ultimate reward."

"But what does this mean for James?"

"Who's to say?" Jael said, "Maybe nothing, maybe everything. It doesn't matter, it doesn't change your mission."

"Yes, yes, of course." Shaerlyn said. She smiled and reached over and hugged her brother.

"I would return it, but the moviegoers would think I'm hugging thin air and worry about this old man."

"So," Shaerlyn ventured "Popcorn, huh? It's that good? James doesn't seem to like it."

"It's that good. Now, won't you keep an old man company and join me and you can try it for yourself?"

"Here? I guess so, but not in this." She pointed at her bronze breastplate and white linen robes.

"It's the 1980s. You can wear what you like."

Shaerlyn thought back to the day before she had seen a pleasant look looking mother wearing a nice floral dress. In an instant, the dress appeared on her and she dyed her hair and eyes to match the pretty mother that she had seen.

"Interesting," mused Jael. "Of all the fashion that is available right now, you chose what? A floral summer dress? We have punks now, punks with pink hair."

"I happen to like it, I guarded the garden. I like flowers, especially these... Sunflowers. I'm not quite ready for some of the other fashion here. Now, listen, Jael. Where have you been? Where do you keep disappearing to?"

Jael sighed. "I told you, Istanbul. I don't go anywhere else. There is someone there that intrigues me and we spend time together."

"Human?"

Jael grinned again and said, "Let's enjoy the movie, shall we? No more questions, let's head back to the physical plane and you can try popcorn at last."

Shaerlyn nodded, but there was something... Something she couldn't explain in Jael's behaviour. She loved her brother with all her heart and she didn't expect him to be evasive, but he seemed to be protecting the person he was referring to. For some reason.

She reached down into the physical world and the Ethereal plane disappeared and her fingers touched oily popcorn for the very first time

***

Superman II was a brilliant film, I really liked General Zod. I still hate popcorn, I don't even like the smell of it. Yuck. Except the coloured type that isn't hot and smelly.

A week later, the first Superman movie came on the TV. It was annoying that we saw the second one before the first again, like Star Wars, but the first movie really captured my imagination. I could see myself running faster than the train to Frankston.

Somehow, deep inside, I knew this was my destiny too. I think my parents are my parents; I don't think I am an alien. I mean, I could be. Maybe my parents are too? My Dad is super fast and my Mum is very beautiful, it is possible.

All I knew, with my black hair and eyes that were sometimes blue or greenish blue, I looked a bit like Superman and I was fast. How fast? I would have to find out one day. I thought about telling James Blundie I was Superman but I needed someone to keep my secret that would be there to help me. And we were moving, otherwise it would absolutely be him.

***

Yesterday was my last day at school, I said goodbye to everyone and Mum told me I could write to James Blundie and visit him when we came to visit my Grandma and Granddad and my Aunts. I even had a cousin, Sharon, about Stuart's age. We were leaving all that behind. If I saw James Blundie again, I would tell him the truth about my powers. So this was all up to Mum and Dad now, but they always keep their promises.

Peter and Amy seemed a bit disappointed I was leaving, but it didn't seem real. Only when Mum took us to the Driscoll's and the sisters there cried with Anne and Margaret that I understood it was all really happening.

Christmas was different this year. I woke up early and rushed to the tree, Margaret said she wanted to be in charge of opening the presents. Mum and Dad got me a Stormtrooper, my sisters and brother gave me a combined present of Darth Vader and Santa got me Luke Skywalker in his X-wing costume. I was thrilled. Grandma and Granddad gave me some clothes, My Aunt Pam bought me socks and my other Grandma gave me a card with $2 in it!

Later that day, we went to the park and met Grandma and Granddad and my Aunts and Uncles. My cousins were there too. Stuart got a bit more attention than me, but I was too busy playing with my Star Wars to care. Mum had to grab me when I went too close to the lake.

Tomorrow the removal truck will come, we are actually going to drive the car up and Dad promised it would be an adventure. He said it was 1000 kilometres, and that sounded a long way. I hoped I don't get carsick.

***

Shaerlyn drifted down to Earth and watched the family depart, new hopes and dreams. The father's new job, mother worried about meeting other mothers, the girls excited. Young James unsure and sullen, a single tear rolling down his cheek.

She walked through the fence to James Blundie's yard and greeted Theonis, that boy's Angel.

"It's been interesting with you as a neighbour." Theonis said and reached over to her and gave her a big hug.

"And to you, Theonis, and all your help these last few years. I trust your next neighbours have a little less drama."

Theonis laughed and stepped into the sandpit, pointing at the ground "So many souls, who knows when one grain of sand will meet another again? If the family comes back down again, remember to visit."

"Of course, brother. Call on aid as needed and do not tarry too long without seeing the throne again. I am sure you are well missed in heaven."

"It has been a while, for sure. Fortunately, I have had an easier job of it than you have. And HE must be pleased with you."

Shaerlyn smiled "I do all things through HIM, he gives me strength. And HE gives it to you too."

"HE does, for sure. Go now, sister. Travel north with them and keep them safe."

Shaerlyn turned around and looked at the house she had been with for the last 5 years, now empty and alone. A new life would begin in Quakers Hill, and she was curious about that place.

With a final wave, her wings spread in the morning sun, and she took to the skies.

3

Chapter 3

Shaerlyn glided down as the Campbell family drove up and parked. She landed on soft, green lawn, allowing the pleasant feeling of grass between her toes.

She had listened in to the family conversation on the way. The house was in an estate for Navy married personal, called "The Patch" or just Married Quarters. Some were on the base proper, but the Campbell house was just outside the main gates.

She glanced around and saw a street full of life, plenty of children here to be friends with James. That was good. She worried how he would adjust to the move, but with other children around it should be easier.

The house was much larger than their previous place, a red brick building with sizable but sparse yard at the back. In the front was a solitary tree. Not one really for climbing, which would disappoint James a bit.

She followed the family inside, Anne and Margaret pushed past their dad to explore and choose bedrooms.

James walked in carrying a box of toys with his father beside him.

The mother came in last, holding Stuart's hand.

Inside was a sea of vinyl and plastic bench tops, tiles throughout. Not a big kitchen but a good size living area. One long hallway led to the bathroom and bedrooms.

The place looked... tired. But it was big, and there were enough bedrooms for everyone to have one each.

After the challenges of their previous life, she hoped things would be quieter from now on and she could monitor James mostly from Asgrax.

She couldn't explain her connection to that world, but 200 years in one place, she had found solitude there and was as close to being as home as she felt. Heaven was always there to welcome her with open arms, and it was incredible to be in the presence of HIM and all her kin.

"Faith increases when the Lord seems far from sight." She said.

The war for souls had taken its toll on her that was true. She needed to see through things with James and for him to grow into a fine young man. But after... another assignment or task? When Lucifer and his Demons were gone from existence, there would be peace... but when? It would be better to rest soon and often, before that final struggle.

Satisfied that everything was fine and James was happy with his room, she slipped through his soulgate and returned to Asgrax to observe from afar.

***

Dad came home from his first day at work carrying something under his arm.

"What's that Dad?"

"Actually, son, it's for your room. It's for you."

"For me?"

Dad nodded and put down his briefcase he was carrying in his other hand and led me to my bedroom.

"I got these from work, I hope you like them." He unrolled a series of posters.

The first one I recognised "A-4 Skyhawks! Wow, cool!"

It was a picture of five A-4 Skyhawk jets flying in formation. Some were camouflaged, and some were white, all had the word Navy written on them.

I looked at the next picture. It was an aircraft carrier. I know this one. H.M.A.S Melbourne.

"This is H.M.A.S Melbourne, our aircraft carrier. You know your Dad was also on an aircraft carrier, HMAS Sydney. But we used it to take troops to Vietnam. We called it the Vung Tau ferry. But this is H.M.A.S Melbourne, she is our only aircraft carrier now, and she is going to be replaced soon by a British carrier and we're going to call the new carrier H.M.A.S Australia. And it is going to fly Harrier jump jets."

"What about the Skyhawks? You told me they aren't fast but they can carry a lot of bombs and they are really, really manoeuvrable."

"Yes, that's right, they are, but they can still break the speed of sound in a dive. The

Harrier jump jet, though, can take off from anywhere, it's called VTOL. Vertical takeoff and landing, and they are also very manoeuvrable because they have engines that move so they can go up and down easily. Maybe you will fly one one-day."

I knew nothing about Harrier jump jets, but I don't want to see the Skyhawks go away. Maybe they could have both?

The last picture was a picture of a ship, with a lot of guns.

"This is H.M.A.S Vampire, those are 4.5 inch guns in double barrels. It has a lot of firepower. It's fire-control radar is so accurate that one time there was a Phantom jet towing a target and the guns took out the target and then started tracking the wire leading back to that the plane. The pilot would have soiled himself that day."

I did not know what soiled himself meant.

"They are based on the British Daring class destroyer. They don't have the 5 inch guns that were on H.M.A.S Perth, my ship that I commissioned, but H.M.A.S Perth only has two guns and the vampire has three and the double-barreled, so pack quite a punch. Actually, James, there was a tragedy a few years ago and H.M.A.S Voyager, H.M.A.S Vampire's sister ship and H.M.A.S Melbourne you see here, hit each other. Many people died. It can be quite dangerous, my job. But I don't go to sea anymore."

"So I can put these on my wall?"

"Yes, that's what I got them for, for you."

"Thanks Dad." I said. It would make my room look better, the blue walls were a bit boring. I was sad that the Skyhawks might be going. But I was also sad about not seeing James Blundie, it had been almost a month and our school was about to start in this new place and I didn't know what I think about that. I hope James

Blundie doesn't forget me. But these posters are nice.

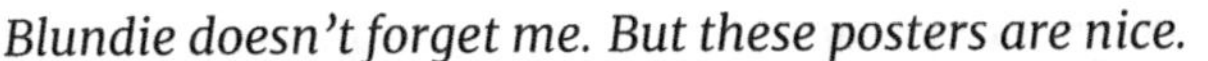

***

It would be tough, and I was nervous but Mum said it would be okay.

"Your sister is going to be on the bus too, if you need anything she can help you."

"Mum, can't you just drive me to school?"

"James, you're a big boy now, you need to do these things for yourself. I won't always have time to take you."

"But can you take me today?"

Mum gave me one of those epic smiles and patted my head "The sooner you get used to it, the better. Now here is the bus. Hopefully, you will make some new friends."

I trudged away to the waiting bus, Margaret standing there like she owned the world. She was so confident and strong!

As the bus arrived, she leaped on and headed straight to the back. I got on and followed and went towards the back, to her.

"Find a seat near the front, James" She said. I stopped confused. We're not sitting together? Then I saw she was already in deep conversation with some other girls from our street. Her new friends. Oh.

I turned around and looked for an empty seat. I found one next to a boy with darker skin. I haven't met many people with darker skin, only seen them in TV shows sometimes. But he was not dark, dark. Just a really good tan or something.

"I'm Andrew."

"My name is James."

"How old are you? Are you in my class?"

"I'm in Grade 2, you?"

"I'm in Grade 1. We just moved here."

"Oh? Where from?"

"Hastings. A little place in Victoria."

"I don't know it. I am from here. But my family is Maltese."

"What's that?"

"Malta is an island."

"You are from an island?"

"No, my parents are from there. I was born here, I haven't been there but I want to one day."

"I want to go to an island too! Will you take me?"

"I would have to ask my parents if it is okay."

"Oh, please do that. Can we be friends?"

"Yes, of course. We can catch the bus together every day."

My first friend here. Still, I kept thinking of James Blundie (and Peter and Amy too. Oh, and even the Driscoll girls.) It was weird here without them. And Andrew didn't live on the Patch with the Navy, he lived somewhere else. Maybe I could ride my bicycle that far to see him?

***

I wasn't nervous about starting this school, and I soon found other friends. Turns out Andrew was more a "Bus friend" because he was a grade older than me at school and already had his friends there. But I could sit with him on the bus and I could visit his house after school. His mum was amazing and served up a heap of food I have never tried before. I know nothing about this place called Malta, but they know how to cook.

I didn't mind not seeing him at school, as I soon found a best friend in Evan. He was older than me; everyone seemed to be, with very blonde hair and blue eyes. He lived just beyond the school and he didn't need the bus. Despite his mother's lesser cooking skills, I spent a lot of time there after school and slept over often.

My teacher's name was Mrs Swords, and she was the most beautiful woman I had ever seen! She had short, black hair and the reddest lipstick you could ever imagine. For Valentine's Day, I made a card for her, but I was afraid to give it to her. When I got in trouble for doing something silly, it devastated me when she told me off. She saw the effect this had on me and later always did it with a smile and soft voice, and then I would do anything to be better.

I wanted her to be my girlfriend. Everyone talked about girlfriends. But other girls smelled funny and had germs. My parents commented once after a Parent–Teacher meeting that they thought she wore too much make–up, but that was ridiculous. She was so beautiful and I wanted her to be my teacher forever.

At lunch time, I would often hunt down Margaret to see what she was doing. She was a senior, and I looked up to her. She would always say hi but I got the feeling that she did not want me around her friends. Just like Andrew and his friends.

Evan and I started a group, and we called it the Vampire Club. Other kids joined us and we hung out near the school fence, in the far corner of the school. There was a tree there, and we wrote our names on it.

At this school I didn't have the same problem with going to the toilet, but I got lots of nosebleeds. No one knew why I got them, and Mum took me to the doctor a couple of times. They just said they would stop eventually, but I hated them. Usually I would try to find my sister, but I spent a lot of time in the sick bay.

***

I knew I was a very handsome boy, my mother told me this all the time. She would never let my hair get long and we would go to the hairdresser's or sometimes she would cut it herself. I certainly couldn't be handsome if I had hair like a girl!

In our front yard, there was a small tree, which I discovered had a nest with eggs in it. I was very excited about this and so when my hair was cut at home; I collected my thick black hair on the ground and made a small nest for more birds. My sisters didn't think it would work and my father told me the birds would destroy it, but surely it was much warmer and better than a nest made from twigs?

So I did not listen to anyone and crept outside and put the nest in the tree. I was sure I would be right and find birds in it the next day. But the next day the nest was gone. Maybe someone had stolen it, or my family had removed it. But everyone denied it. I never forgot this though and how I wanted to help the birds, but others didn't believe in me and that my little nest of hair would work.

4

Chapter 4

I am not sure when Theresa came into our lives. In one moment she was there, her Royal Highness, the Princess of Persia.

I've never had a pet before, and I don't care what my sisters say, she was my cat. Not our cat, mine. I love running my hands through her long silky hair and I play with her every morning, long before anybody else wakes up. Mum told me that if she was to be my cat, then I would be responsible for feeding her and cleaning up a little box. I didn't listen to my mother; I knew someone else would do it. This is a lesson I am learning fast. My sisters seem to love working, I don't have time for that. I have toys to play with.

Our family was well represented in competitions, already. I won the giant Easter bonnet parade for an enormous hat that Mum and Margaret put together. Still, it was me walking around the circle and beating the other kids.

Next, was Theresa's turn at the pet show, held in the same quadrangle at school. She got second place and lost out to a dog. I didn't really understand dogs and why people like them, they just bark all the time and sometimes they scare me. I mean, some look good and Dad told me he used to have a dog name Sam, and he had loved it very much. I don't know why Sam isn't here, but Theresa is.

Anne won a singing competition and got a second place in the javelin. My sisters were always off doing sport and even Mum had taken it up. Sometimes, on Saturdays, Mum and the girls go to netball and I have to come along too. It is pretty boring but usually I get a Fanta. Still, playing with some Lego next to Theresa is so much better, and I don't understand why I can't stay home with her. I am going to be 6 next year.

***

Cats were always a problem. One of the great mysteries that her King never revealed was that cats had keen eyes that could see into the Nether and Ethereal plane. Thus, they can spot angel and demon alike, and liked neither. Why they had this special skill was a mystery.

Thousands of years before, in ancient Egypt, Lucifer himself sat on the throne and used cats as guardians to alert him to any angelic presence. It meant now, she usually had to watch passively from across the street as Theresa made it known, the house was her domain.

Only Jael, when he visited, seem to have some sway with the feline and explained that his absence was to see a friend in Istanbul, a city with a plethora of cats. If the cats didn't take to him, there would be no place in that city to hide. Fortunately, Jael had some way to smooth the path to Theresa's heart. Indeed, Jael could sit with Theresa for hours and seemed to converse. Shaerlyn simply lacked the ability.

She wasn't the only one frustrated, her angelic kin who protected the rest of the family , regularly sat on the ground opposite the house, frustrated. Still, it was a pleasant break. It would be only one more year or so before she would have to match up and fight Ki Koa again.

James couldn't be called a baby any longer, not with that temper. At school he seemed to earnestly try to be the centre of attention at all times and was often disruptive in class. Still, his teacher, Mrs Swords, had the patience of any in the heavenly realm and he seemed to respond well to her.

Out on the playground, James and Evan recruited others to the little club who would hang out by the big tree at the corner of the school. Club activities centred mostly around climbing this tree. Still, James found himself in trouble with some older children and got into the habit of kicking them in the shins and running away, trusting his speed to evade capture. He soon learned that his best chance was to quickly find Margaret who would beat up anyone attacking her younger brother. James was impressed with this, and Shaerlyn much less so.

As it was Easter in a few days, the family was getting ready to go camping near Nowra. This had been where his parents had met and the family lived before Hastings. So it was a tradition, almost every year, to climb to the bottom of Tirinjara falls through the forest, on a path most didn't know about.

James had only been there twice before and didn't remember either, and they both had been uneventful. The first time, baby James was only two years old, carried to the bottom of the waterfall on his father's back.

The biggest development was that Theresa wasn't coming and would be fed by a neighbour. That meant Shaerlyn could watch James uninterrupted.

***

There was something about the Australian bush, something ancient. It was as if it existed in a time before the rest of the world. There was its beauty and there was terror.

Shaerlyn felt a mixture of emotions of both elation and unease. It was like the Bush was its own entity, always watching. It could offer up sustenance or malevolence.

The family had gone on their annual trek to the bottom of Tirinjara falls which required only mild exertion for the most part. Now the mother and the girls and young Stuart were up at the campsite, getting a small fire going for dinner.

James was walking with his father and was peppering him questions about Bush Craft, survival and if there were going to be any rabbits to shoot.

The father led his son to a small creek and pulled out pan and explained to him how to find gold.

Suddenly a scream rang out from behind them and birds took to the sky. The father turned in a flash and scooped up James and ran back towards the campsite. Shaerlyn darted ahead of them.

More screaming and Shaerlyn focused on the direction of the noise, to see Haniel and Netzach towering over the scrub and looking tense, like they were about to draw their weapons.

Anne was screaming, and she was hardly one for hysterics. What was it? And then Shaerlyn saw. Just a foot away from Anne, and in striking distance, was a serpent. A shiny black snake flicking its tongue and meandering closer to Anne's feet.

What came next surprised even Shaerlyn. Bursting through the bush, still carrying James, the father leapt onto the scene. He put James aside, pulled out a mighty knife from his belt and snatched up the snake in one quick movement. He moved the snake a metre away and lowered to the ground, still holding it just behind the head, and then placed his boot there. Then his blade sawed off the head, and he held the snake up triumphantly.

"It is a red bellied Black, nasty thing. Very poisonous. Anne, are you okay?"

Anne didn't answer, but in tears ran back towards the campfire and her mum.

Shaerlyn raised an eyebrow and looked at her angelic kin, who were just as shocked as she was.

The father turn to James and showed him the snake "We can cook it up for dinner tonight, don't worry there is no venom anymore."

James's eyes were as wide as the moon as he stared at the shimmering light off the scales.

***

It didn't taste like chicken at all. It was tough and chewy like I was eating a shoe. Mum, Anne and Margaret refuse to even try it, but Stuart ate more than the rest of us, even Dad. Stuart loved food even more than I did.

Still, it was quite cool that you could eat almost anything out here. Dad called it bush tucker and told me this is what the aborigines ate. I think I preferred steak.

Anne had been going on about the snake for the last hour, Margaret was largely silent and just patting her on the back. Normally Margaret was the talkative one and Anne never said much, unless she was singing. She just loved to sing.

***

We got back from Easter holidays I was a chance to go back to school. I was looking forward to seeing Evan again, his place was a bit far for me to visit. Sometimes I would visit him after school as he lived just beyond it, it was actually near where my sister Anne went to school. Anne had some friends near the school too, and sometimes Mum would come and pick us both up and bring us home after a few hours.

But school meant something else to me. Mrs Swords. She was just amazing, always smiling at me and encouraging me, even though I was slower than some of the other boys. She was so, so beautiful. She had dark hair like Mum and I think that one day I would like to girlfriend with dark hair. Well, I wasn't sure about girls but Mrs Swords... If the girls in my class looked like that, but they were all just so silly.

Dad had brought the snakeskin home and hung it on the back fence to dry. I think he was going to do something with it, but after a week Mum threw it out.

We live right next to the Navy base, HMAS Nirimba. My father is an instructor there for the Navy apprentices, dealing mostly with the radios or something like that. Most of the time he seems to be doing sport, and he always comes home late because he was training himself or coaching others. One day I hope he would coach me to run fast. Well, I could run fast, but I want to run faster.

He doesn't use the motorbike very often and I would sit on it; he told me it could be mine one day. I have never been so happy in my life; I love that motorbike.

I would wake up early every morning to play with Theresa but she never seems happy about me waking her up but it is nice just the two of us in the morning while Dad is snoring, Stuart is probably dreaming about food, and I don't know what Mum or my sisters get up to. It is a private time, just me and Theresa.

5

Chapter 5

The dark cavern had what appeared to be a wall of old broken television screens. There was not a more rancid place in all of Hell, and Gulya struggled to even enter.

She felt his presence immediately, green floating eyes in the dark.

"It's been a long while since you graced me with your presence."

"Trust me, I wouldn't be here unless I had to be."

"The great Gulya doing the beck and call of some other demon? Must be some demon."

"It is. You want to be on the right side of this. Changes are coming soon."

The gaseous black cloud floated up to her "Changes have been coming since Lucifer thought it was a grand idea to go for the scroll and take on Heaven itself. I just go where the currents take me. Into the hearts and minds of the humans."

Gulya nodded "That's exactly what I'm asking you to do, a special favour."

"A favour for you? I will pass."

Resisting blasting him across the room, Gulya said through tense lips, "No, not for me. For Ki Koa and the chained one."

"Oh, that is interesting. Certainly seems wise to accept. Sure, okay, you want to watch the action from here?"

"I'm in Hell already. I don't need to be punished further."

"Well, rude and predictable. Who is the target?"

"James Campbell of Quakers Hill, New South Wales, country and continent of Australia. The boy, not his father."

"Well, I'm intrigued why he has the Dark Lord's attention, but I will get to it right away."

"Your services are noted." Gulya said.

"Yes, well, one more thing. After this you will owe me, you personally. And you supply the bodies."

Gulya grimaced, but she would not protest "Very well. I will owe you." She didn't fancy scooping up souls from the pit "And I will supply the bodies."

The demon floated past her, just glowing green and angry eyes. His name was the same in all languages. He was Nightmare, and tonight he planned to fix on the mind of his prey.

***

Some surprises Dad gave us were amazing, some weren't fun at all. He was always trying to trick me and thought it was funny. Like when he told me that Ice cream vans play 'Greensleeves' when they are out of ice cream. But I could see the other kids and I wasn't stupid. Okay, it took me a few weeks to realize.

Another joke he played on my sister Anne. We don't normally go to restaurants; they are too expensive. But we went one time to a restaurant and the table next to us ordered these things called oysters. Dad whispered to Anne that the next table were eating them wrong that you had to close one nostril and then snort the oyster up your nose. She totally believed it.

When he ordered some oysters, he gave some to Anne who then went to eat it the 'proper way.' Only at the last moment, as Anne's nose was about to hoover the plate, did he stop her and tell her he was joking. He thought it was hilarious, Mum scolded him too. Why does he do it?

But today's surprise was amazing. We all got in the car and drove for a few hours, and we all had no idea where we were going. If Mum knew, she didn't say.

And then we were at this city mall and there there was a Tardis! What! I loved 'Doctor Who' so much, we watched it every night as a family and even Dad would try to get home in time to see it.

Then I saw K-9 the robot dog from the show, coolest dog ever.

A group of people, all ages, were crowded around... curly hair and scarf...it couldn't be? It was, it was! 'Doctor Who'! The real 'Doctor Who', Tom Baker.

My dad had brought me to meet 'Doctor Who'. Did he use the Tardis to come from England? I even got a card in the shape of the Tardis that Tom Baker signed for me. Best day of my life!

So, sometimes, I like Dad's surprises.

***

Shaerlyn was back on Asgrax and swimming around a rock pool. Nephis had left, but Farida was still here, singing her song at the mouth of the cave into the wilderness. The melody was sweet, and some of the mighty and forgotten on the planet fled to the far side.

Farida's song bubbled through the water as Shaerlyn swam in the resonance and peace. As she swam, she looked down to see the mother put James down to sleep and tucked him in, telling him it was too late to listen to a story from the 'Magic Faraway Tree'.

All was quiet, always good. Cathor was imprisoned, and even Ki Koa was still a year away from being released.

***

Gulya hated nothing more than visiting the pit. It was the noise, the screeching and screaming of writhing bodies being torn apart again and again.

It was a vast pile of flesh that descended for miles, all crawling over each other. Deformed and swimming in what couldn't be blood but certainly looked the same. A bath of blood and bodies.

She opened the creaky iron gate and stared over the abyss of humanity, the stupidest creatures in the universe. The only creatures willfully blind to the spiritual world and embracing their ignorance.

It was one big cosmic joke. She knew what she was and the decision she made but humanity closed its eyes, blocked its ears and raised the middle finger to the obvious truth. Now some of them would leave the pit for a day to be the engine of Nightmare's toying.

She looked at the list. Five murderers. Made sense, they were people of action and Nightmare needed some of those. Twenty embezzlers, thieves and Wall Street bankers. Nightmare needed people with some imagination. A few randoms, an adulterer, two elephant poachers and an arsonist. No paedophiles, even Hell had standards, and they didn't leave the pit even for a day.

She stepped into the bloody fluid, grabbed a hook lying on the pit's edge and began to drag out the bodies one by one. It was hardly a pleasant task, and the screaming seemed to only intensify. It better be worth it. If Nightmare failed, she would have to do the work herself, and there was no worse smell than that of man.

***

Mum reads the best books and I think Enid Blyton is my favourite writer. Three books capture my imagination more than anything–'The Magic Faraway Tree', 'The Wishing Chair', and 'The Boy Next Door'. Mum says I've stayed up too late watching television, and I have school in the morning. No story tonight. And I am quite disappointed.

As I drift off to sleep, I feel strange, I have a tightness in my chest and then I think I hear a voice.

"Sleep."

The voice doesn't seem friendly, and I try to open my eyes but I can't and then I begin to dream.

The dream starts as a memory from a time I don't remember when. There is a park, a big park– there is a lake and my aunts are there and my cousin Sharon and her baby sister Joanne. And one of my Grandmothers is there and so is Granddad and I love them both so very much. I think I am Granddad's favourite, actually I think I am Grandma's favourite too. It is a beautiful sweet dream of sunny skies, good food, running around and all eyes being on me.

And then there is a shadow across the sky and a mosquito lands on my arm. I slap my arm and squish it. Then another one lands and then another. I kill them both, then I feel more landing on my head, landing on my neck, drawing on my blood.

I stand up and dash around and run even to the lake and throw water on my head. Mum runs towards me, worried that I would fall in, but I am just trying to get the mosquitoes off me. Then more and more mosquitoes seem to stab at me, and I feel pain all over my body. I scream and scream.

Mum and Dad wake me up. Mum tries to reassure me but Dad seems annoyed and I couldn't understand why. He is there in just his underwear.

It was a nightmare, I couldn't help it. Why did he seem angry with me?

After a few minutes, my Mum leaves and I close my eyes again.

***

Nightmare hovered over the boy, his first attempt interrupted. He lowered himself onto the boy's head, becoming dozens of flies and then hundreds, crawling over his face, up his nose and into his mouth. Flies flooding into his throat, choking off the boy's air.

And then from behind him he heard a hiss, and he turned and saw a cat snarling at him.

***

Shaerlyn paused in the water and stared down at hissing Theresa. In an instant, wings sprung from her back and Shaerlyn dove through the soulgate and landed in the room.

She saw James's face going blue, mouth gaping as flies flooded in. His eyes were alert and full of fear and hands flying about, not understanding what was happening.

Shaerlyn launched herself across the room and spoke a word, and the creature was flung from the boy. She grabbed it and ran through the wall outside.

"Nightmare." She said with disgust.

The demon solidified in her hands and pushed himself away. His body was a grotesque distortion of naked humans writhing in pain. Souls from the pit that he could carry along with him for a time and use their energy to bring terror into the dreams of man.

Now outside, Shaerlyn could draw her sword and slashed down, cutting the demon in two. But nightmare merely reformed, and all she had achieved was greater screams from his meat wagon.

Nightmare struck back, leaping onto Shaerlyn, and wrapping bodies and bodies around her. Squeezing, poking, punching, biting. Shaerlyn dropped to one knee under the fury of the assault.

And then a sound, the sweet sound. Farida was here.

Nightmare was thrown from her like a concussion wave, and Farida stormed after the beast as Shaerlyn tried to recover. She looked behind her and saw Nightmare at the edge of the yard, howling and wakening the neighbouring dogs. But Farida's voice served all but evil, and she broke into another song. A song of revelation, song of the End of the days, the song of the rapture.

Nightmare scurried along the grass, trying to find any relief as Farida stood over him and pulled out a chain. Without missing a note, the chain went around a limb of the beast and in moments Uriel reached down and snatched the demon away.

Shaerlyn and Farida were all alone in the backyard now.

"Bless you, sister, but how?"

Farida's note died away, and she smiled "I felt your anguish so I rushed back to the rock pool and saw you were gone and peered through and saw you fighting the demon. What happened?"

"Demonic attack, they used the demon Nightmare to attack James in his sleep. The poor boy must be terrified."

"I might be able to do something about that." Farida said.

Farida walked back and helped Shaerlyn up, and the two walked through the wall to James' bedroom.

James was coughing and crying and was sure to alert his parents.

"Relax." Farida said, "I can manage this."

She sang a Psalm, one she had composed with David. The Lord is my shepherd, I shall not want.

And with that, a cup of goodness and peace filled the room and all tension and anxiety left the Campbell household. The household fell into deep slumber.

"Thank you, sister." Shaerlyn said and gave Farida a warm hug.

"Is it always like this? I worry about you Shaerlynel."

"Seems to be, but I can't fathom why this child has so much attention."

"I guess the why doesn't matter. Whatever our father has in mind for this boy, we can endure through HIS strength."

"Amen. I'm going to have a walk around the house."

It was then that Shaerlyn noticed the cat, Theresa. Not hissing, trying to rub against their legs. In vain, because they were incorporeal.

"Seems like you have a new friend." Farida smiled.

"A nice surprise, she seems protective of James too. Perhaps she realises we are on the same side?"

6

Chapter 6

My dreams last night were strange. I was in the middle of a nightmare and then I wasn't. I was suddenly walking through the fields behind the Driscoll house back in Hastings. Just Dad and I.

By early morning I had largely forgotten it all and focused again on school.

School is so much fun. I really like all my classes with Mrs Swords. She is such an outstanding teacher, and I always try to sit at the front of the class in our lessons. Sometimes I even fight the other boys to sit in the front. I think they like her too. The only class I don't like is painting.

I am not good at it. I really, really struggle and all I want to do is to make a beautiful painting to show Mrs Swords. But I am so bad at it. She is a patient and kind, though. Still, my paintings often are a disaster and sometimes I will just tear them up and throw them in the bin.

"James, you mustn't do that. It's art. We all have to start someplace, even the greatest artists had to learn like you are. Keep going."

That was what she used to say, and it helped but after a few months of trying, I was getting very frustrated and sometimes I would even cry. A boy named Steven *made fun of my painting and I threw paint at him. He started crying, and it felt good that this happened to him. But then Mrs Swords appears, and she just looks at me with disappointment in her eyes, and I couldn't handle it anymore. I run out of the room and keep running all the way across the quadrangle to the tree where our Vampire Club meets. I climb the tree and sit there as I watch Mrs Swords look around for me but I am so embarrassed, so ashamed and I just stay in the tree for I don't know how long. I am really starting to think I will live in this tree when I see my Mum arrive through the front gate and head towards Mrs Swords' classroom.*

"Mum," I call out.

"Oh, James. I was worried sick about you. Come down from the tree."

"I can't. Mrs Swords is mad at me."

"She isn't. She is just worried about you. Come on, come down and we can go show her that you are okay."

"I'm sorry, Mum." I slowly climb down from the tree.

"I am just glad you're okay." She gives me a big hug and pulls out a tissue and wipes away my tears and then holds my hand and brings me back towards Mrs Swords' classroom.

***

Everything became better at school, and I even got better at painting. And then the worst day.

"James, it's going to be okay. I promise."

"No, it's not! It's not fair!"

"Dad has to... We have to move because of Dad's work. Dad's work is important, isn't?"

"What about my friends? What about Evan? I'm not going to see him again."

Mum put her arm around me. "He can come visit us or we can visit him. And you can always write to him."

I am not impressed. This is the same as what happened with James Blundie. We moved, and they told me we would see him again. But we didn't. And now we're going to move again.

"Evan is my best friend. Please, tell Dad we can't move."

"James, listen to me. Dad is in the Navy and his job is important. This is good for his career and good for all of us. Your family. You will find new friends, and hopefully we will be there for some time."

"How do you know that? Maybe in another year we will move again?"

"Maybe," Mum said, "But things will settle down soon. When we get to Canberra, you will get a new bike. Your bike is getting a little too small for you now. You're becoming such a big boy."

"I don't want a new bike. I don't want anything to change. Maybe you can go to Canberra and I stay here with Evan?"

"You really want to stay here and be without me? That would make me sad, James. I want my beautiful son to be with me. Don't you want that?"

"You've got Stuart." But when I say it, I see the pain in Mum's face. It was a silly thing to say, but I was angry. It upset me. Of course, I don't want to be away from Mum.

"Okay, James. I have to check on the girls and Stuart. You stay here in your room and play with the toys. When tea is ready, I'll come and get you."

Mum stands up and walks out of the room, gently closing the door.

I am alone, alone again. It isn't fair. At least coming here was a bit of an adventure. And I met Evan. I am still sad that I don't see James Blundie anymore. Does he even remember me? I don't want people to forget me. I don't want them to have new friends. I don't want Evan to have another friend. I am his best friend. I don't understand why we need to move, just because Dad's got a promotion.

I sit down on the floor and started to build with my Lego, but I can't imagine anything and can't decide what to build, and I soon got bored. So, instead, I climb into bed, cry a bit more and go to sleep.

***

Dad had promised an adventure. We aren't going by car, so how will we get to Canberra?

At the back of the Navy base, is an airfield and sitting on the tarmac was a Hercules. A C-130 Hercules of the Air Force.

I had packed all my toys up and actually packing was fun. Theresa would go with the boxes and the car and motorcycle too.

We get out of the Navy van and board the plane at the back; the seats are along the side and they give us big ear muff things. Then the door close, and the plane starts to move. It is very exciting but also very, very noisy and gets noisier as the plane takes off.

We are not in the air for long; I am not allowed out of my seat and I can't talk to Anne next to me; it is too loud. We land and are met with another van that drives us through the suburbs. I think it took longer than the plane trip.

And here we are. Macquarie. The new school is directly across the road, which means I wouldn't be late and no bus to catch. Big front yard, but not much of a backyard. Even not one, but two trees to climb.

I get the end room opposite Mum and Dad. I can't wait for our stuff to arrive for all my toys and to put my posters up again. I hope Evan can find this place when he visits.

7

Chapter 7

I have been at the school for a few weeks now. It's not like Quakers Hill. The school was just across the road, but somehow that made me late almost every day. I don't know why. When I was at Quakers Hill, catching the bus every day, I was never late.

My teacher's name is Ms Masters, and she seems nice enough but a bit grumpy. We have a really fun game called 'who stole the cookie from the cookie jar' and I get excited and always want it to be my turn. Ms Masters doesn't like that.

I miss Mrs Swords. She was so much better than Ms Masters. Ms Masters is okay and I have some new friends. First, there is Dominic. Dominic lives just down a little laneway from my house, not far at all, and I go there often after school. He has an Atari with 'Space Invaders', but he only has one controller and we often argue about who can play. He also likes Star Wars and has so many, even including the X-Wing fighter. I am so jealous.

There is another boy on my street called Nathan and I like him too, and he has a trampoline in his backyard and a big dog. I go over there sometimes. But most of the time, I spend with Dominic.

There are two girls at my school who are really nice. Elizabeth and Belinda.

Belinda's last name is Campbell. Like mine, and I ask my Mum if she is part of our family, but Mum says no. That's good, because I like Belinda, but maybe I like Elizabeth more. I didn't like girls before, but they are pretty and Elizabeth is funny and she seems to like me.

Actually, there is a boy at our school named Craig who looks just like me, and his birthday is one day after mine. Many people get us confused, but he has more freckles on his face than I do. Strange, but we aren't best friends. You would think we would be the best of friends, but I spend most of my time with Dominic playing video games and playing with his Star Wars.

I have my own Star Wars too now. Our things were delayed and so we had no toys, so my parents went and bought us new ones and I got several Stormtroopers, a robot thing that was a bounty hunter and even a Jawa. I wanted to get Boba Fett, but I couldn't find him. I also got Luke's land speeder and this gun that looks like a radar that if you press a button, it falls apart like it exploded.

***

I can't believe it. It was great that our things arrived from Quakers Hill. Theresa too. My Star wars toys, my posters and everything else. But one thing was missing.

The Motorbike! Dad just said, "Oh, I sold that before we left." WHAT! I tell him he had promised it to me when I was older and he says he didn't promise but I know he did. It was normal for Dad to miss certain school events and things, I am used to that. It is because of his job, but this is the first time he truly disappoints me. I don't think I can ever forgive him. Not unless he goes back to Quakers Hill and gets it back.

Then things get worse. There has been a gigantic pile of sand dumped on the edge of our block, probably because we are on the corner and they are working on the road. Dominic, Stuart and I would play in the sand and played there with my Star Wars toys and Dominic's too. It was like the desert world in Star Wars.

Dominic had to go home and didn't want to carry all his toys, so he left them there and I left mine as it was getting dark. I would collect them all in the morning or just leave them to play with them tomorrow after school.

But the next morning, as I was rushing out the door late again, I saw the sand was all gone. All my Star Wars, all of Dominic's Star Wars, were gone. I ran into the house and began crying and rushed up to Mum and told her.

She came outside and said, "Oh, James!" and looked down the street and saw the workmen who were working on the road. She told me I had to go to school, but she would speak to them.

That day at school was really hard, I didn't know what to say to Dominic and, of course, Ms Masters was angry at me for being late.

When I got home, Mum had Dominic's X-wing, my Darth Vader and two Stormtroopers. The rest were gone. Plus a lecture about always bringing in my things at night.

Dominic came over and Mum explained everything to him and he was crying too and rushed home with the X-wing, without even talking to me. I couldn't blame him. I think I have lost him as a friend now.

***

On Earth it was the early days of 1982, but in Hell, time always seemed to stand still. This was where Shaerlyn was near right now, hovering over the pit- the fortress of the damned.

She didn't think in Earth time…she thought merely in the time until Ki Koa's release, and of course Cathor's later on. It was still a few months away, but she spent a lot of time here, watching the dance as the demons flew from Hell, released from seven years imprisonment. The angels would hover (indeed she countered at least forty near her) awaiting the demon they so imprisoned to come forth. Then the pursuit would begin.

The demons were cunning and did not always appear at the moment of their freedom, but rather wait till more than one was freed, then fly out together. There was nothing more frustrating for a demon to be caught outside the very gates, and nothing more satisfying for an angel to achieve this. Once a demon left the confines of the planet itself, it was far harder to catch-especially with soulgates nearby.

Baby James was soon to be seven years old and despite being awkward as a child, his heart was that of gold. He was always inquisitive and had a rich imagination. He had a tendency to lie and make stories up, which was of some concern, and indeed he was bored easily. But Shaerlyn felt he was on the right path, a seeker of the truth, and his eternal placing seemed to be with his mother, who was a fantastic role model for him.

Still, as much as she missed him, Shaerlyn spent more and more time outside the gates of Hell. Her last encounters with Ki Koa and Cathor had wounded her. Those scars of sin were long gone, but the memory remained. She could have failed. Failed the boy, failed her King and fallen. She would not take such risks this time.

She felt an angel hover next to her, but she did not glance at him. She thought back to her time in the middle kingdom, China. What an adventure that had been! She smiled to herself. The colours, the flags always flying in the breeze. The politics and oh, the suspicion! A young boy, forbidden to marry the woman he loved, fighting for her hand just as the nation faced the growing threat of the incoming Mongol warlords. She could always admire such spirit, and she asked herself if being somewhat romantic in leanings was something common and correct for angels? Surely she must care for man and who she has in her protection, but the human emotions of fighting for the sake of a loved one- to give up all to be with the one you treasured- was this thinking, ideal? Certainly she saw the parallel with her own King and the choice HE made for sacrifice, so surely if HE chose this path then it was one of virtue? How could an angel emulate this?

She remembered what she had done already for young James, and perhaps some of it had been reckless, like to not shield his eyes to the supernatural until much too late in his life. She had corrected her mistake, but it had sent baby James into the hospital. Was she selfish at that time to spend more time with the baby? Could it be because of her isolation away from humans she longed to be near them?

The time in China was certainly different from now; it ended well-unlike with Jean her most painful memory in France. It was too early to say for James. How would this end? All she could do was her upmost to keep the stubborn Ki Koa and Cathor away. Young James, ultimately, would make his own choice.

She turned now back to the present and glanced at the angel beside her. Glaudos! She could not believe it.

"Glaudos dear brother," She cried "What brings you here?"

Glaudos beamed at her "I was wondering when you would notice me." He chuckled and continued, "I did a small errand a few years back, well of course seven, and so I have to keep myself busy every seven years or so. You know how it is."

Shaerlyn laughed "Oh yes, actually it is a bit more frequent for me. With two to handle,"

"Ah yes," Glaudos said "So, how goes that?"

"Well," Shaerlyn began "It wasn't so long ago I caught that imp- you remember the one from Asgrax?" Glaudos nodded "-But Ki Koa will be out soon so I am just preparing for that."

Glaudos smiled "It seems incredible how you bested a seraphim on your own."

Shaerlyn nodded "Well, of course, I do all things through HE who strengthens me."

Glaudos sighed. Shaerlyn looked at him puzzled.

Below them, the iron gates began to open.

Shaerlyn asked, "Your turn?"

"Yes, yes," Glaudos answered "They like to have a welcoming party when I am around," He continued to grin "It is time sister for me to head down there. Would you care for a closer look? It could be a good experience for you."

Shaerlyn considered, but she had no desire to be closer to Hell than she was. When the time came, she might dare, if it helped catch the demon. But not now.

"No, not at the moment," Shaerlyn said "So tell me who is guarding the throne room with you away?"

Glaudos looked perplexed for a moment. Shaerlyn frowned at his slow response. Glaudos finally said, "Sorry, I was concentrating on the task at hand. We will talk about it later, okay?"

Shaerlyn smiled back at him "Of course."

The gates grew wider.

"Time to go" Glaudos said, and he reached for Shaerlyn to hug her goodbye.

Shaerlyn responded and put her arms around her brother, but the moment she did so she knew something was wrong.

She tried to let go, but Glaudos held her fast. Then she felt something bite at her skin. Then the nausea. She felt needles on her back and Glaudos' hands seemed to claw into her.

"Something wrong?" It was an amused voice and one which echoed through all eternity. That voice. THE voice, that foul and evil serpent.

She tried to tear free, but she was held in an iron grip. She looked up and Glaudos' face was no more, a swirling mist of blackness and rot.

Lucifer.

Her blade ignited, but she was held in the hug so tightly she could not wield it. The surrounding angels cried out and charged, but the Devil was too quick and dove towards the opening gates, dragging Shaerlyn with him.

She fought him; she fought the beast, but it was useless. She screamed as his sin started feeding into her. She could hear his hollow laugh as the wind rushed around them. As their speed increased, angelfolk trailed behind, green eyes flashing vengeance for a millennium.

"The devil may appear an angel of light" She had not been vigilant and not taken heed of the scriptures. Glaudos would have been one of the last to leave the King's side for any mission or errand. She had only seen him on Asgrax after the great call out to Michael. Oh, where was Michael now? Could her angel kin rescue her? It seemed not, with the gates of Hell mere moments away. She called out to her Lord.

The Devil snarled.

They landed just inside the gates. The gates began their slow movement to close. She looked around as best she could. Thousands upon thousands of demons were before her. Behind them were the writhing bodies of the damned, the condemned humans. Wailing at their pitiful existence.

Lucifer became his true form beside her and bowed, still clutching her hand "On Mars, I welcomed you to Hell but I was doing you a disservice, a poor facsimile. So I felt it only proper to invite you here. Welcome to Hell, Shaerlynel! I hope you enjoy your stay."

8

Chapter 8

Lucifer released Shaerlyn and threw her to the ground. The demons around went into the throws and cries of ecstasy.

Cerberus , the hellhound, bounded forward and blocked her escape to the gate. Slowly, she rose to one knee and glanced around.

The first thing she could feel was the true absence of her King. It was the most awful feeling that this place seemed to exist without his presence. Indeed, behind an inner gate lay the hordes of the damned, their bodies constantly ripped apart without the will of the Great I AM to hold them together. She could hear their screams, far worse than any of the fallen on Asgrax as more and more tumbled from the giant soulgate above the pit. The only one no angel of goodness would pass through. She realized Asgrax had HIS presence muted somewhat, but here was a true absence. The difference was stark.

Black charred metal walls enclosed this place, with demonic archers on the parapets. This might be where they were outcast to, but the gates had been breached two thousand years ago in Earth time, and it wasn't to happen again.

Slowly a crowd of demons formed a circle around her, still wary of her still lit blade. Lucifer stood legs apart and proud over her, his height towering and blocking much of her view.

The great prince of Hell touched his mirrored breastplate, where Shaerlyn's sword had once struck "You did this" he said "And there is no redemption in this place".

Slowly the demons came closer and suddenly her wrists and ankles were grabbed. A demon she recognized as Golgus, slipped a brutish arm around her neck and then whispered vile obscenities about her King, into her ear, just to see her struggle.

Her sword could do nothing, with no way to wield it, and she allowed it to disappear. Cerberus eyed her hungrily.

Even the cries of the damned seemed to quieten with such a spectacle before them.

There was laughter from the watchtowers as angel after angel threw themselves at the gate outside to rescue one of their own. Foul arrows of sin flew down onto them, and for a time the angels retreated. No doubt word would reach the angelic host armies soon, but the gates of Hell were strong, and numbers were on the side of the fallen. Shaerlyn's fate seemed sealed.

***

Sarcogus, the jailer, knew what had occurred above. He could not intervene himself. The sole angel who dwelled in Hell, his mission was to keep the demons imprisoned in that very state. To leave the lower levels, then, was unthinkable. But he could not abandon Shaerlyn to the horde.

Ki-Koa was delighted when he had heard the news and shook the bars on his cage. Sarcogus walked past, but not before smashing his fist into the Demon's face, and sending him flying to the other edge of his cell.

There was only one thing for Sarcogus to do. It had only been used once before.

Sarcogus moved into a run and pounded down the corridor to the other end. Before him now was a small chest, it was a smaller version of something once carried by the Israelites.

Inside was a golden horn. He pressed it to his lips and blew.

***

Jael was standing alongside Ruzanna, on a rooftop terrace overlooking Taksim and Galata, with glimpses of the Bosporus in the distance. He heard the call and looked skyward.

"You must go?" Ruzanna asked, touching his shoulder.

"Yes, I must. My King. Something has happened."

Ruzanna sighed and met his eyes "Come back soon my angel."

"I will, I promise." Jael said, transforming into a majestic winged horse.

"Oh, that's a new trick! Be gone my winged warrior and do not tarry but come back to me!"

The horse bowed before her and took to the skies.

***

Michael was upon the Earth when he heard the call, guarding Israel's northern border with a dozen others.

Gabriel was on the other side of the galaxy, travelling through a soulgate back from Earth, after conveying a message to a Minister in Fortaleza, Brazil.

Raphael was in Heaven alongside Nephis, and they quickly reached the armoury as the first archons lined up for spears and armour.

Farida was on Asgrax, looking through the soulgate at young James, quietly sleeping.

The doors of the great temple opened, and the choir filed out briskly, without a sound, and took up arms.

In a few moments the army was assembled, thousands of archon spearmen, with bronze helm and breastplate. Four thousand chariots, with fire for wheels and filled with archers and the mighty cherubim and seraphim. Winged archon pegasi waited, ready to pull them into battle.

The host and the horde had fought many times. The numbers seemed against them. But the horn had been blown. Neither the angels nor their King forgot their own.

From the open temple doors came an almighty wind, and a cloud so bright and magnificent appeared. Upon it stood a figure filled with such glory it was impossible to look upon.

The saints came forward, led by Peter and Elijah.

"Your numbers are few," Said David, one of them. He had once been a mighty king and ruler and his war against the Philistines was legendary "We know how to fight."

The saints climbed aboard the chariots, alongside angelfolk, to fight together for the first time.

They would succeed. The gates of Hell would not prevail.

For the Son of Man, himself, would lead the assault.

***

There was a call from one of the guard towers and Lucifer turned. Shaerlyn struggled on, but Golgus held her tight.

Lucifer climbed up to the top of the tower and peered out. No!

"Archers!" He called.

The demon horde mobilized in an instant and sped up to the parapet.

The purple-grey sky changed, like it was lit by a thousand suns. Blazing chariots swept down from the clouds, full of the angelic host. Could this be the final battle?

And then the sky grew even brighter, and seemed to disappear, and Lucifer felt his body shaking. His knees buckled and the other demons called out to him.

Coming into view now was a cloud alike no other. It growled thunder, with lightning streaming out from it in every direction. As it came closer, it seemed to fill the sky. Upon it was a lone figure, with a golden sceptre in his hand and eyes that ripped into Lucifer's very being. The Son of Man.

Arrows flew as the chariots came near, the demons recovered and shot back, projecting their filth over the walls with deadly accuracy. Angels swerved away. Below the fortress of Hell, below the very escarpment, lay the lake of fire and the end to any who fell in it.

Lucifer laughed as the attack seemed to falter, but the presence of the Son of Man unnerved him, as that cloud continued approaching.

"Bring forth the ballistas." He barked, and they obeyed his orders. Huge crossbow-like weapons spat forth huge flaming arrows that crashed into some of the angel chariots, which disappeared out of view towards the fiery lake below.

"Yes," Lucifer cried, thrilled that the capture of just one angel could lead to his victory "Press on! Imp spearmen to the gate!"

But he failed to give more commands, because there was a sudden scream, as the Son of Man opened his mouth. The words were ancient, the very words used once to create all things. The words all must obey, for all is made by him.

"Open." Said the words in that old tongue, and from the Son of Man's mouth, a giant red-hot sword appeared and grew, growing enormously and stretching forth to the front gate.

"Nooooo!" Again Lucifer cried and commanded the imps to form up and prepare to defend their ground.

But the glowing sword, reaching from the horizon smashed the gate apart and took out the first few rows of imps. They vanished instantly.

Lucifer climbed down and ordered the rest of his troops to battle, as the angels , seeing the way open, edged ever close and circled the walls.

"Catapults!" He called out. As he ran past Shaerlyn, he turned for a moment. Her eyes were filled with joy. The Devil stopped and swung a jeweled glove into her face.

She took the hit well and said, "See you soon."

Lucifer ignored her and grabbed onto the nearest catapult and pushed it forward. Other demons joined him, knowing their fate if the enemy attack succeeded.

***

Michael and Raphael arrived at the gate and, using spear and shield, broke through the first waves of imps guarding. Jael came behind, sending arrows up onto the parapet, protecting those two from the sky above.

More streamed in and a beachhead was established, but the demons had the advantage of the tower walls to rain fire down on the incoming angels and the assault again slowed.

It was at this time that Shaerlyn decided it was time to make her move. She had no intention of allowing Golgus to let go of her, instead she transformed into a pillar of holy fire and held him.

The demon's flesh burned away as he fought to break free. Shaerlyn smiled and spun out of his grip and lit her sword. The demon stumbled back and felt the blade enter him. His hands instantly clutched around it and his eyes grew wide.

Shaerlyn pulled out her chain and swung it around his neck. In a moment, the great angel Uriel appeared and dragged him below.

Shaerlyn turned to Lucifer. Their eyes met. Lucifer did not grin. Shaerlyn showed her teeth and charged.

The devil stepped away from the catapult, pushed an imp out of the way and came at her. Half into his run he became the monstrous dragon again, and his troops cheered.

Shaerlyn stood firm, her sword passing from hand to hand in anticipation. This was it.

***

The angels broke through the rows of imps, only to find themselves outnum-bered by the demons waiting behind. Slashes of fire cut into their ranks and they fell one by one, under the heavy assault. The demons pressed them and forced them back.

Jael saw the dragon charge towards Shaerlyn, his dearest friend all alone. He leapt over the surprised shoulders of Michael and ran over the heads of the first three rows of demons and jumped free, speeding towards his sister in trouble.

His bow appeared, and as the Devil lunged at Shaerlyn, he spied the gap in the dragon's mirrored breastplate and fired.

Three sacred arrows shot out from his bow and two hit the mark. The dragon collapsed forward and roared in pain, his body sliding over the dirt, his body thrashed about. Slowly he rose to one knee.

That was when Shaerlyn struck, slamming her sword into the dragon's eye, she leapfrogged over him and a golden chain swung out from her , which slipped around the beast's clawed leg and snapped shut.

The battle stopped. Even the damned were silent.

Almost quietly, Uriel appeared at their side and yanked the devil away on a chain.

The angelic host cheered, the demons retreated back in the chaos. The angels, awaking from slumber, poured in and sent more to imprisonment. But the victory would be short-lived.

***

A horde of demons stormed the prison, and Sarcogus could offer little resistance. The gates to all but one cell were held tight by his command, and there was nothing the demons could do to pry open them. So he let the demons pass.

Uriel appeared next to him with the thrashing Lucifer and they descended together. The Devil spat and swore, trying in vain to change form again and again. Arrows still protruded out of his breastplate. He was no longer in dragon form.

There were shouts below, and as they descended, Sarcogus glanced at Uriel. A fight was breaking out downstairs, at the deepest level of the prison. The cell designed for Lucifer himself.

The Devil dragged his feet like the coward he was, but the two angels used their enormous strength to propel him forward. Obscenities spewed from the Devil's mouth and Uriel laughed. Perhaps the first time the Angel of Death had laughed in a thousand years.

They reached the bottom level to a scene of a battle. Demon versus demon. Inside the large cell here, there were the remnants of the battle. Five demons and an imp lay on the floor, some only just moving and twitching. Two demons remained and were busy unshackling a monster between them.

Sarcogus paused for a moment and looked at Lucifer beside him "Somebody is not happy."

At the dawn of time, before the fall of man, his own had imprisoned this demonic prince. Imprisoned for suggesting even a course different to that of Lucifer.

The angels had held him not, for such imprisonment is for only seven years, but enough demons can imprison one of their own for eternity. But now this demonic prince was free, and staring at his former jailor, the ever jealous, the ever envious Lucifer.

"Lucifer." He said.

"L'edor." Snarled back Lucifer, struggling on his chain.

L'edor poked the Devil in the breastplate, circling around the arrow wound "I will be back," He said and punched the Devil in the face "But for now I am going to do right what you failed to do for so long. Finish the humans once and for all and stop this cosmic chess game."

L'edor strode out, flanked by the two demons. Lucifer felt the chain being fastened to the wall.

"No one can hear you here, Lucifer" Said Uriel, setting three quick jabs into the devil's chest. Sarcogus came up next, his enormous eyes glowing. He swung his head down into a headbutt and sent Lucifer back against the wall. They stepped out and closed the door, leaving Lucifer to his fate alone.

***

As L'edor walked past Ki Koa's cell he paused "You will be out here soon, my loyal servant."

Ki Koa grinned and shook his fist in triumphant.

***

Le'dor collected an army as he rose to the surface. Demons dropped their allegiance to Lucifer at the very sight of him. The demons and imps rallied at his call and his swagger became a march, his march began a run and his run became a charge.

Shaerlyn saw the mass of demons coming at them, outnumbering them three to one. She cried out, and Michael and Nephis called the angels back.

"Everybody outside!" This time it was Gabriel, Shaerlyn hadn't noticed him before.

Shaerlyn broke into a run as the first of the demons threatened her. Now was not the time to fight. She stumbled and slid along the ground as two demons grabbed her. She kicked them away and scrambled to her feet, but another demon yanked on her hair and dragged her to the hellish floor. Her sword appeared, and she cut the foul being in half.

She rose again as trumpets blared outside. She could peer through the gates and could see a chariot awaiting her, with one of the dear saints, the peaceful Francis, beckoning her.

She got up again, and an imp flew at her; she used the butt of her sword to smack him in the face. A tall, purply grey demon grabbed her around the shoulders and pulled her back half a step. Another slid a hand around her neck. She felt claws in her eyes. She tried to transform into a pillar of fire, but they were expecting it and transformed themselves into gaseous clouds of repugnant gas–trapping her inside. Her hands swam through the toxic fog, but she could not advance.

Suddenly the sky lightened around her, waves of wind kicked at her and the demons screamed. In front of her stood one lone Angel, Jael, firing volleys of arrows at the oncoming horde and sending holy arrows into the cloud around his dear friend.

Shaerlyn, coughing sin, took a step forward then almost fell again but took another step.

"Come on!" Jael said, arrows flying from his fingertips in smooth motion, his bow burning brightly as it fired.

Shaerlyn saw her friend smile, almost a sad smile. Shaerlyn glanced up and saw the awaiting chariot. She could feel her King just beyond the walls- it lifting her up, encouraging her. She began to run. There were screams behind her. She sprinted forward, past the gate, and leapt for the chariot, grabbing Francis' outstretched hand. The chariot spun and shot away, and she collapsed on its floor. There was another Angel here too. Was it Klaudos?

Slowly, she climbed to her feet and looked back at Hell. Her king had spoken a word, and the rock face grew into a new gate that was slowly closing.

***

Tears were in his eyes as he fired his arrows at the onslaught. Seventy-three demons lay at his feet, but more kept coming. But he had saved his friend.

Le'dor stood before him, such a gigantic monster of a demon that he was. Jael smiled, remembering the millennium he had served his King. His arrows bounced off the grand demon, much as they would Lucifer, save the weakness in his breastplate. L'edor grabbed him and pulled off both his arms.

The huge demon grabbed Jael by the head and threw him over his shoulder, towards the sea of squirming humans.

A memory of salted air and seagulls, deep eyes and a soft hand. Istanbul. Ruzanna.

Jael disappeared into the pit of cursed humanity.

***

Shaerlyn climbed off the chariot. She couldn't even face Francis. The other angels were celebrating the glorious victory, the great rescue, and they rushed up to hug her and she just stood there. Jael. Jael was gone.

Like a dream. She wandered through the crowd of saints and thought about the cost. The folly, how Lucifer had tricked her and now angels were gone. Jael was gone! Probably fallen already consumed in sin-could she face him on the battlefield? It was all too much.

Tears in her eyes. she walked away and yearned for Asgrax exile once more, well, self-imposed exile. As she wandered, she looked up and saw Abdul guarding the scroll room as he always did, and then...

Her fists clenched, and she pulled her sword and ignited in the air, and she stomped towards the scroll room. Her eyes alight with fire.

Abdul step towards her. "Don't, Shaerlynel. Don't!"

"You might see a moment into the future, Abdul , brother, and best anyone, but I have the sword that none shall cross. Out of my way!"

Abdul step back as she flung open the doors and faced the scroll. The universe. She looked down to the bottom right corner and saw where the parchment was alight. Hell.

Behind her. she heard Gabriel call out, "Don't Shaerlyn please." But Shaerlyn reached forward and touched the flames, and in a moment was once again outside the gates of Hell.

Other angels were hovering in the distance, still awaiting any escaping demons. Shaerlyn ignored them all and charged at the gate with her sword.

The demons on the parapets noticed her and arrows came down, but she was fast and her sword reached the gate and struck it. But nothing happened.

She swiped, she slashed, and she yelled and she banged on the doors with her fists.

"Let me in! Can you hear me, Jael? Jael!"

She heard the angels behind diving down to retrieve her, but she would have no one else fall this day. With fury and frustration, she took again to the skies and left the doomed place and soared into the cosmos. Away from her kinfolk and to be alone in her thoughts. She was broken.

***

The sunset lit the scene and plunged Sultanahmet into a silhouette of a former age. As she gazed across the waters of the Golden Horn, Ruzanna knew Jael wasn't coming. Something had happened. Her gaze lowered and a single tear rolled down her cheek.

"Farewell my angel. Let this not be goodbye."

9

Chapter 9

ad was nursing something special in his hands. He called the whole family to the lounge room and opened up a box, and it was a VHS recorder. Wow! As an added surprise, he got a special copy of a movie not available on VHS to everybody, but available to the Navy.

He set up the VHS recorder and explained now we could record our favourite TV programs. It took a while to connect everything as Dad refused to look at the instructions.

Then we sat down, the entire family, as he placed the movie in the VHS. It was the story of 'Conan the barbarian'. Dad explained the main actor was a bodybuilder but I don't know what that is. I have never seen so many muscles. Muscles on muscles like that. Dad also has muscles, especially on his arms, back and legs. But this actor Arnold Swarcelnegga, Shwortsineggaer- I can't say his last name-this actor has huge chest, not as big as boobies some girls but big. Much bigger than Dad's. Maybe I could be a Barbarian AND Superman? Oh, I wish we had this VHS recorder back in Quakers Hill when Superman came on. I would watch it every day if I could.

***

She smashed asteroids with a word. She sliced them apart with her sword. She pounded them to dust with her fists. It wasn't enough.

She dove through the gas clouds of Jupiter. She rode comets in the Oort cloud. She travelled to distant worlds where diamonds fell like rain or glass came in on the wind. She travelled further and further, twisting time and space around her. Beyond the soulgates and any quick passage home.

She stood on planets full of primeval soup and steaming volcanoes. On any of these she could have made a command and life would have emerged, just as Lucifer had created his hellhounds Taetus and Cerberus. More life in this universe? It was all like losing Jean 200 years ago. A staunch believer who died in the mud of Waterloo and cursing God's in his last breath, condemning himself, and his family falling into ruin after him, without their father.

It broke her then, and this broke her now. They had come for her, to rescue her, but so many fell and Jael-why did he even come? He was in Istanbul and Shaerlyn long suspected what that meant. But he had come and sacrificed himself. Now he was gone.

At best, he would be tortured until the End Times but keep his soul, but far more likely he had joined the ranks of the fallen and would soon be the archer of Lucifer. And she might have to face him. She couldn't.

Time went by and she didn't know how long she had been out of the cosmos, but then, what seemed to be carried by the solar wind then resonated through the rocks,was a song.

Farida, Sweet Farida. Her voice travelling even here. Farida, who was left watching over James.

It was the thought of James that made her eyes look earthward, though it was out of sight. James. She had a mission, an obligation, and more-a love. For that clumsy, cheeky, mortal boy, and this is what Jael would have wanted. This is what Jael sacrificed himself for- to save her so she can protect the boy as her king had deemed.

Could she do it? Doubt burdened her. And grief. Had not HE said to give HIM your burden, your yoke, so that you would find rest?. Yes. Yes. She went down onto one knee on an unnamed world and prayed.

"Our father, who is in Heaven,
    Hallowed be your name.
    Your kingdom come
    Your will be done,
    On Earth as it is in Heaven."

Afterward, she roared through the cosmos with purpose true anew. First to Asgrax and to Farida and then back to young James. It would be her way to honour Jael.

***

And Le'dor appeared above the British fleet with a macabre grin upon seeing such destruction.

And as Exocet after Exocet slammed into the fleet, he cried, "Burn, burn, burn!" and fanned the South Atlantic wind with his might wings, till aluminium and steel ignited and burned.

As the men prayed for their souls, as ships fell beneath the waves, he laughed at the pathetic fighting prowess of man. Building weapons of steel and lead, unaware of the actual battle waged for their souls.

***

Tears welled in her eyes. She couldn't believe it.

In her humble cave, on Asgrax, was not only the beaming Farida, but Nephis, Kapyrol, Gabriel and even Michael. She fell down on her knees and sobbed, and the angels rushed towards her and pulled her to her feet and embraced her.

"Our sister is among us!" Michael said. Michael, she could not believe Michael was here. He had armies to lead, Israel to protect, yet he was here, for her.

"Have I disappointed you? Have I disappointed... Our father?"

Michael smiled. "Well, a few of us are wondering what happened to a few asteroids, but no, Shaerlynel, you didn't disappoint us. We all grieve in our own way and we will miss him, we all miss Jael."

"I've been helping Farida a bit while you've been away." Nephis said. "But she has been doing a splendid job, really. But the boy, James, needs you."

"How is baby... How is James?"

Farida said, "He's fine. His sister, Margaret, tried to go backwards down a hill rollerskating and ended up in hospital. You should have seen James, I was so proud of him. I mean, a week ago, Margaret was chasing James and James didn't know that a glass door was closed and ran into it. He was fine, just surprised. And not hurt. Still, while Margaret was in hospital, he sat beside her. He even prayed. He has a great love for his sister, even though they fight so."

"And Margaret is okay now?"

"Yes, Netzach got there just in time to cushion some of her fall. She's already moving around and will go back to athletics soon. She may not roller skate for a while, though."

"Well, this is all so much, thank you all. Right now, I really just want to see James again."

Michael patted her on the shoulder. "Of course, dear sister. Back to work! All of us, let's return to our stations and await the day of our glorious victory."

The angels cheered and wings were outstretched and they took to the skies one by one, some to soulgates and others into the cosmos and a journey to the beyond.

***

The mother poured tea and placed some scones on the table "Jim, we really need to talk about James. His behaviour. "

"He's fine, love. Just strong willed."

"Jim, he is getting in endless trouble at the school and is struggling. He's smart enough but is always playing up to get attention."

"What do you suggest we do?"

"Well, you are going up to see your mum next week. I really think you need to spend some time with him. He is sensitive and never sees you with all your sport and commitments. He hero worships you."

"You want me to take him along? I don't see why not. Might be good for him. Bit of an adventure. Like when we used to hunt together."

"Exactly."

"Sure, no skin off my nose. I will teach him about life, the birds and the bees and all that."

"Jim, he's far too young for that. Just be there for him. I know he will love it."

"Consider it done."

***

As the bright birds of day nestled in their nests for the coming evening, as bat and owl took their place in the sky, Shaerlyn flew North. As deep rays of sunset abated over Canberra at the curtain of night consumed all, Shaerlyn was where she belonged. In the air.

Below, a sole vehicle, a golden brown station wagon sped North, leaving city lights for country roads on the long drive to Brisbane, over 1000 km away.

She had been surprised upon her return to see James' dad announcing a car trip with just him and James. She had heard stories that L'edor was loose on the Earth. Dangerous times, but whether at home or away, she would stay by James' side and protect him. Even a short time away, mourning the fall of Jael, had meant she had missed so much. She would not fail James, she couldn't, not now. For Jael and our King!

***

So great to spend time with Dad, I don't see him that much. He is always doing sport and comes home about 7:30 which was close to my bedtime.

Usually, we only see each other on the weekends, our camping trips or wardroom dinners. Wardroom dinners are a strange affair. Everyone starts the evening very polite, Mum would wear a pearl necklace and a beautiful dress. Fellow officers would come up to me, patting me on the head and tell me that I would make a fine officer one day. I didn't like being patted on the head, even by Dad.

After some beer, port or wine is drunk, all the officers are very loud and often dance about in a silly way and sing songs from Gilbert and Sullivan or a very rude song, according to my mother, called 'Barnacle Bill'. I don't understand the words, but everyone thinks it is hilarious, except Mum.

Now we are going on a trip, just Dad and I. He has a friend in Brisbane who used to be in the Navy but is now a painter. His name is Gordon but what is interesting is that he has a son named James too and Dad told me he was named this after me.

I am curious to meet him.

My Grandmother, my dad's mum, also lives in Brisbane. I met her a few times; she was blonde like my father. She even came to Tiranjara falls with us when I was very young.

It will be nice to see her but to be honest, being around old people bored me and all I have are a few golden books including my favourite ' The little train that could.'

I don't know why we are driving at night, but Dad says we have to be careful because dusk is a time for kangaroos. Apparently that is bad, but I don't understand why and I don't ask. But Dad tells me to look ahead and see if I can see any.

It is strange leaving Canberra, leaving Mum, my sisters and my fat brother. It is a Saturday night, so we would miss 'Hey, hey it's Saturday' a show we watch as a family. We won't be home until Wednesday, so I would miss a few days of school and my friends there.

Still, I am in the front seat of the car. Dad has the map between us and a thermos of coffee for him and a big bottle of cordial for me.

I don't know why, but when the high beam comes on, there is a blue glowing light on the dashboard above the speedometer. This fascinates me and I just stare at it, but the view is better in the backseat.

As we leave the city, we are the only car, and in the other direction there are nothing but trucks. Lots of trucks. I begin to count them aloud.

The convoy of trucks reminds me of the movie 'Convoy' which I've seen almost as much as 'Blazing saddles'–a favourite movie. Dad is super proud of his VHS recorder, but he told me the Betamax was actually better. We don't have many videos, so we watch them again and again. 'Convoy' is what made me fall in love with trucks and seeing them all now, lit up like Christmas trees is just beautiful.

And there are just so many of them, I count over 300 of them before Dad says "James, you have to stop. It is like counting sheep and it's putting me to sleep."

I don't quite understand, but I don't count aloud anymore and I sit in silence until I finally close my eyes.

***

I wake up, and it was already morning.

"Welcome back to the land of the living." My Dad says. Sometimes he says things I don't quite understand.

"Dad, where are we?"

"We passed the border while you were asleep. We're in Queensland now, just a few hours to go."

It disappoints me to not see the border. I pick up the map and try to study it. I love maps and seeing all the different routes you can take.

Dad picks up his thermos, shakes it, frowns, and put it down. He gives an enormous yawn and rubs his eyes. He looks tired. He looks at me and asks, "Do you want some cordial?"

It was green cordial, my favourite. "Yes please."

"Where's your cup?"

We have these shiny metal cups that we always drink out of on road trips and when we are camping. Been so long since we've been camping.

"Here it is." I scoop the cup off the floor and he seems to inspect it before carefully opening the cordial bottle with one hand while still driving with the other.

"Hold the cup, James. Hold it steady."

His eyes dart from cup to the road and back again as he pours.

"James! Keep it steady!"

We hit a small bump, and I drop the cup and cordial splashes all over the map and my Dad's leg.

My Dad says a bad word and suddenly I feel the car go sideways.

***

Shaerlyn saw the car careen across the road and acted.

She tucked in her mighty wings and dove through the dark clouds- atoms and electricity igniting on her form as she fed more of herself into the Ethereal plane to garner more speed.

She reached the car and flew beside it and put her hands out to touch the metal.

And then Kapyrol appeared at the front of the car, his graceful form holding onto the bumper and wheel arch, his legs spinning backward to match the car's speed.

"I have got this." He said "Protect the boy!"

Shaerlyn nodded and slipped into the car and wrapped herself around young James, whose eyes were transfixed on his father as the father tried to regain control.

She heard a thud and then felt the car slow. Kapyrol had done it.

***

I can't believe it, we almost crashed. Because of my spilt cordial. What did we hit? We hit something. I looked over at Dad; he had a strange expression on his face.

"Are you okay, Dad?"

He looks at his hands and slowly turns his face towards me "Did you say something James?"

"I said are you okay, Dad?"

"No, no. Before. I swear I heard I have got this. Protect the boy. That wasn't you?"

"Um... I don't understand, no I didn't say that. What do you mean?"

"I swear... Never mind. Are you okay? I think we hit something. I was sure we were heading over the bank, maybe we hit a rock or something and it bounced us back

onto the road. It is a miracle. Stay here."

Dad turns off the car, takes off his seat belt and gets out. I watch him circle the vehicle. This could have been terrible, not for me. I am Superman, Dad's strong, but I am not sure he has my powers. Would I have been able to save him? I replay the car going off the road in my head. I imagine if I can get out of my seatbelt in time, reaching over and shielding him with my body. Maybe it is a situation like this that would teach me how to fly and I can fly out the window with him and save his life?

Dad comes back in a few moments with one of those white posts that mark the edge of the road, the ones with the reflector on them.

"I've got a souvenir son. This is what we hit; maybe it bumped us back onto the road. We'll keep it as a trophy."

I just nod. What would have happened to Dad if the worst happened and I haven't been here ready to save him? I just know that I could have, even though it all happened so fast.

Dad gets a cloth and wipes up the spilt cordial and then pours me some more and I drink it. He waits for me to finish, asks if I need the bathroom, then restarts the car and we continued on.

***

I am excited after such a long drive to meet Dad's friend Gordon. He seems quite an interesting man. He has many paintings on the wall. All of them done by him. Some are of birds and some are of simple Australian scenes of old towns. Old banks, old schools, and old houses with children playing, an old man reading a newspaper on the porch.

His wife, Shawna, is full of energy and big, big smiles and gives me big, big kisses on the cheek. Her hair is like a lion. I like her.

James, the son, I thought we would be instant friends, but he seems quiet and doesn't want to be in the room with us. I can understand that, I can be shy too, but still... I'm a James. We have to be friends.

Dinner is a lavish roast. I love roast dinners, especially with gravy. There are some yellow things on my plate that look a bit like lemons. I pick one up and try to squeeze it.

Dad and Shawna are talking, and I don't want to interrupt them, but I am squeezing this thing and no juice is coming out.

"Dad..."

Dad turns and sees what I was doing.

"Dad...what is this? How do you get the juice out?"

Dad gives me a serious look "That's a squash. You need to squash it, just squeeze harder son."

So I do.

"Jim, you're terrible!" Shawna says and Dad, Shawna and Gordon start laughing. The only people not laughing are me and their James.

Shawna sees I am getting upset and says, "Your dad is such a joker. It is a vegetable, you have to cut it to eat it. It's not like a lemon."

"Oh." I say, embarrassed.

We stay there the night, and I show them the post we hit from the road, but it is dirty and Dad suggests we keep it in the car.

***

The next day we go and visit Grandma. Grandma Campbell, Dad's Mum, is someone I haven't known very well. My other Grandma and Grandad I see almost every year, but this Grandma lives further away and she lives alone. Well, she has a really cool fish tank, and a dog named Linda. She isn't a big dog and I like her a lot. Grandma has a small yard at the back with a greenhouse in the middle with plants that Dad called orchids. There is a big mango tree and Grandma had a shotgun and chases away the possums that are trying to steal mangoes. Dad thinks this is hilarious because we are in the middle of the city and the neighbours must think she is crazy. I don't think it is crazy; we hunt rabbits, why wouldn't Grandma hunt possums?

There is a big painting on the wall which I really, really like and it turns out that Dad painted it when he was younger. I don't know exactly what it is, but it is like a fiery dragon flying. Every time I look at it, it looks different; I really like it and am very proud of my dad. He is not as good as Gordon, but I like it anyway. I don't think I can ever paint.

The only thing I don't like about Grandma's place is the toilet is outside, up the back, and sometimes there are spiders there and you have to check to see.

Grandma's place is small and there are no toys here, but I brought some along but nothing special. I was still sad about losing my Star Wars toys.

What Grandma does super well is make cups of tea, which are not with sugar and milk but with condensed milk. I love condensed milk; it is one of my favourite things in the world, up there with coconut ice and licking the spoon when Mum is making a cake or lemon meringue pie.

Grandma is very strong, and I try to arm wrestle her, but she beats me. She has blonde hair and beautiful blue eyes full of life. I don't know what she is. Maybe my powers come from her? She is old, but she still cuts trees with an axe, hunts possums and uses the lawnmower.

***

I have never heard the lights and sirens of a police car before, except the movies, but on the way back home to Canberra on an empty, boring bit of road, a police car chases us.

For a moment, I don't know what we are going to do. In the movies, the bad guys always speed up and try to run away from the police. But Dad isn't a bad guy. We are just rushing to get home to see 'Doctor Who', we missed one episode on the way up and we don't want to miss another.

"Let me do the talking, son."

"Yes, Dad."

We slow down, pulled off the road and wait and I keep turning around trying to see the policeman coming. He takes ages until he is finally at a window. My Dad winds it down.

"In a bit of a hurry. Are we?"

"Sorry, officer, was I speeding?"

"Just a bit." The police officer looked into the car through the window and sees me looking up at him. I really don't know what to think. His uniform isn't as impressive as a stormtrooper, but he still has a gun.

When he looks at me, I feel very guilty and can't stop myself "Just trying to get home in time for 'Doctor Who'."

I can hear a groan from my father and there was a moment of pause and the policeman chuckled, "You're a 'Doctor Who' fan, are you? Who is your favourite doctor?"

"Dad says there's only one real doctor, he just changes, but Tom Baker is the best. I met him."

"You've met 'Doctor Who'?"

"And K-9. K-9 was there, wasn't he Dad?"

Dad added, "He did a special appearance at the mall in Queanbeyan."

"Okay," said the officer. "You are very lucky to meet 'Doctor Who'. I wish I had met 'Doctor Who'. Who's 'Doctor Who''s number one enemy?"

"The Daleks!"

The policeman leans back and says to Dad, "You've got a good boy, I'm going to let you off with a warning. But please, no more speeding, even to see 'Doctor Who'."

Dad nods at the officer, starts the car, and we drive away.

"I know you said don't speak, Dad. But he liked 'Doctor Who'. See? Everybody likes 'Doctor Who'."

"I told you, that I was going to do the talking. You are lucky, he seems to like 'Doctor Who'. Maybe he didn't. And when you told him we were going fast to see 'Doctor Who' I couldn't pretend that I wasn't speeding. It could have been a big fine for me. And that would mean less money to buy toys, okay? Please, when I say I will do the talking, in the future, I want you not to say anything. Got it?"

I don't understand. I thought I was being helpful. Now Dad is mad at me. "Yes, Dad." This is the worst trip. The rest of the way home, I say nothing.

We arrive back in Canberra in time for 'Doctor Who' because Dad still drive a naughty way. But I don't want to see 'Doctor Who' and go straight to my room and don't have dinner either. Mum comes in, worried. I just tell her I feel sick from the car and I don't want to go on long trips again.

Back at school tomorrow.

10

Chapter 10

We had just seen the movie E.T, and I cried. My sister thought it was cute that I cried and told everyone. The worst was that she said it in the cinema and my parents and other sister all looked at me. It was none of their business. It was an amazing film though, I especially like the start with the spaceship and also when the bicycle flew through the air. I wish my bicycle did that. I won't forgive my sister for telling everyone that I cried. Never, ever.

***

L'edor unleashed Leviathan to strike at the Argentinean naval forces steaming towards the Falklands. He turned his attention to the British forces, clapping his hands with glee, and fanning flames with each Argentinean strike over subsequent weeks. The Atlantic Conveyer met its end along with landing ship Sir Galahad.

Then from the heavens, with a wingspan more than a mile across, came the great angel Phanuel, known as the face of the Most High. Once the protector of the lands of the north- from Scandinavia to Kievan Rus, to the principality of Muscovy, he was now guardian of Ceres and a young Stuart Campbell. He came as a two-headed eagle and with giant claws snatched up L'edor into the sky, into the cosmos and away from the world of men. The battle over the islands would occur without demon prince's further interference.

***

Yesterday was an amazing day. It was so strange how it happened, really.

The school bell rang, and it was time to go home. Now often I ran instead of walking home, the need to do this difficult to explain. I ran along a concreted walkway, fully knowing there was a row of steps ahead. Perhaps I was distracted, I don't really remember what I was thinking about, but I was certainly not concentrating on what I was doing.

So then I found myself flying, the earth betrayed me and fled from my feet. It took moments to register that I had ignored the stairs and kept going, oblivious to any danger. The feeling was quite amazing. I had my school backpack on, however it did not seem to limit me.

But now I felt something else, a quiet fear and nervousness, as I peered down at the earth insisting I join it once more.

My legs peddled the air, as the third step from the bottom informed me that was where I was to land.

My eyes closed in that second, as just one foot hit the step. As it hit, I pushed with reflex and flew up again, propelling myself forward. I landed with a perfect, fluid run, like what I did was both normal and natural. I could not believe what I had done, and yet I was accelerating away from the scene.

I heard someone say "Wow, he really is Superman!" and at that moment I knew it was true.

***

With the story of my incredible leap spread, there was an air of expectation I would repeat my performance. The next day I looked at the stairs I had leapt from and still could not believe how I had jumped down them, and the feeling of flight realised. I didn't need others to tell the story; I was singing the tale to anyone who would listen anyhow, and indeed by the time I came to class many were talking about it (but of course not as many as I would like).

So now I was compelled to do it all again. This time, I ran with no bag, watching the opening maul at the edge of the stairs. I was focused, concentrating hard on the ledge and when to leap for victory. There was quite a crowd gathered to see.

My speed matched the day before, perhaps faster still, and I launched myself into the void boldly and with cheers. Like before, I seemed to fly, but the nervousness appeared sooner and I glanced down at that same at the third step from the bottom. My foot reached down to touch it, but my body followed too quickly after, and my entire weight fell on that ankle. Bang! My ankle twisted, and I somersaulted headfirst into the concrete path.

There were cries of concern, there was laughing too. People rushed forward to help me as I cried and sobbed in pain. A teacher came and told me how foolish I was, how dangerous it was to do and with my pride smashed, I hobbled home.

***

A few weeks later, I was at my friend's Warwick's house. He had the most marvelous trampoline, fully Olympic. Being the size I was, I had to climb up even to get on it.

Now that I knew I was Superman (and this was no secret thanks to my mouth), Warwick and I played a game on the trampoline where he would be Lex Luthor and I would be Superman and try to catch him.I had hurt myself on the stairs but that was because I didn't land properly and even Superman has to land properly.

So now we stood opposite each other on the trampoline, and I was ready to spring. We both had silly grins on our faces. I launched myself into the air.

***

Shaerlyn sensed the danger and sped to Earth as fast as she could. If only she could get there in time.

***

Warwick was fast and ducked away easily. I landed near the edge and had to bounce a few times to get back into the centre and recover my balance.

Convinced I had him this time, I jumped again, with all my might, straight at him.

This time he dropped to his knees, and I flew over his head. My body kept going, and I went over the side, head first. I didn't even have time to be afraid, just felt an awful sensation as my head aimed to kiss the ground.

***

Shaerlyn reached for James, to perhaps use herself to cushion the fall momentarily. It was going to be too late. Now everything rested in the hands of her King and his will, for surely young James' head was going to smack into the ground and his neck snap in two.

***

My hands were out in front of me, in some weird attempt to stop my fall. I shut my eyes and might have even prayed. It all happened so fast. I felt a sharp pain run up my legs as my feet slipped into the springs and caught me. Everything stopped, but my arms continued forward and my left hand banged against the ground. The rest of me laid hanging in the air, held by my entrapped feet.

A dull pain started to then radiate up from my left wrist, a throbbing ache that put me into shock. I heard Warwick jump down and slowly help me to the ground as tears flooded my eyes.

I wasn't sure about these tears; they didn't even seem real, and I probably put them half on for show. Warwick's mother was soon there to comfort me and led me away.

My legs were a bit sore and Warwick and his mother examined them and it really wasn't my wrist hurting the most at all.

***

Shaerlyn looked on at young James with pity and sympathy for his pain. She had been too late, but the boy survived. She knelt beside him, wanting to comfort. But Warwick's mother was doing a splendid job of fussing and was the first to suggest the arm could be broken.

***

I had just left Warwick's house, and I was still sobbing and had begun to nurse my arm. Warwick's mother called me back and bandaged my arm, just in case, and told me to head straight home.

When I got home, Mum gave me a hug and some warm Milo chocolate drink and told me I didn't have to go to school tomorrow. Of course, she also told me I had to be more careful.

So the next morning I awoke with delight, the arm really wasn't that sore at all, and I got up and watched cartoons.

My favourite, 'Secret Squirrel', was on at 9am which was after school had already started. It thrilled me to be able to watch it and decided I should have a sore wrist as long as possible.

Over the coming days I moaned and complained each morning, insisting the pain wasn't getting any better. Finally, my Mum took me to the hospital, and it was right at 9am when 'Secret Squirrel' was on! Not fair!

It was quite a surprise, considering my acting, that the doctor told me after the X-ray that I had a fractured wrist and would need a cast for six weeks.

I thought yippee! And more time off school, but I was told I could go back to school the next day, wearing the cast. I couldn't believe it!

When I got home, I begged Mum again for more time off school but she said I was perfectly fine to go with my arm broken in a cast and sling.

It was a few days before I could have people write on it, but I liked it when they did. I even did a swastika because I thought this was really cool and that my family were half German and the Germans had the best tanks (Tiger tanks were great) and the best planes in World War Two. I watched all the movies with my Dad and I always wanted the grey uniformed Germans to win.

But my parents were not pleased with this and told me to cross it out and cover it. I didn't understand why. I really liked it because I had it coloured red in the background, and everything else was just black signatures.

Even my father told me it was an evil symbol and that people did not like it. I still didn't understand though.

One thing I found hard was eating, I always ate the opposite way to everyone else. My father said I would grow out of it (just like they said about me having my elbows on the table which was a big no-no) but I still ate like a left-handed person.

So eating was difficult, the other thing was the cast got very itchy underneath, and it was annoying to shower with a bag over it.

I showed my brother Stuart; it was quite a source of pride for me. I confided in him everything about it not really hurting and the reason for this. It was simply because I was Superman and this was just pretend. I even entertained the thought of being Wonder Woman, but my brother didn't believe this for a second, so I stuck with Superman. Still, I enjoyed watching Wonder Woman on TV. My Dad said that my mother resembled her and this made sense (with me being Superman).

When the six weeks were over, the cast came off and my arm felt weak and strange. It seemed so much smaller than the other, and I was told I would have to be careful with it for a while. They gave me the cast as a present, only cutting underneath it to take it off. It was a nice souvenir. It was good for things to go back to normal at school and be able to play with the other kids, but I missed being the celebrity with the broken arm and everyone begging to sign it. Now to break my leg, that would be really cool.

***

I stared at the big box.. it was a train set. It wasn't Star Wars. I looked at my parents, silently conveying to them 'Is this it?'

But they were beaming at me and so proud. I couldn't say anything, but I was trying to not show how disappointed I was.

"Thank you." I said and stood up and carried the box to my room. I liked trains, of course everyone does, but I wanted Star Wars for my birthday, to replace those I lost in the sand.

Well, the train set would be okay for now, but if my parents don't understand, perhaps Santa will. But that is six months away.

Maybe I will like the train set, it depends how long the track is.

***

"I bring news, dear sister." Gabriel said.

"Speak, brother. News from the throne?"

Gabriel shook his head "I know the loss of Jael has been hard on you, Shaerlynel. Alas, Ki Koa has escaped our forces and is free from Hell. You should expect him and be ready."

"We will." Farida said. "Won't we, Shaerlyn?"

Shaerlyn walked towards the rock pool and stared into it. She could do all things through HIM. HE strengthens me. "Yes, we will wait and when they strike, I will chain him again myself."

This seemed to satisfy Gabriel, who took a bow and walked towards the entrance of the cave. "You have the love of our father with you Shaerlynel, never forget. And with that, more power than any of the forces of evil can muster. I need to go, I have errands on earth, but I am not far away."

"Bless you, brother." She hugged him tight then let him go. He took to the skies, disappearing into the haze of Asgrax.

Shaerlyn turned and saw Farida with a curious look. "What?"

"We will be ready, won't we?"

"We must be." Shaerlyn said.

***

October of that year brought another exciting event to the house. The Common-wealth Games. They were like the Olympics, but smaller. The best thing is they were held in Australia, in Brisbane where my Grandma lives. We watched it on the TV, though.

Dad's two favourite people , Robert de Castella the Marathon runner who he trained with, and Kenrick Tucker the track cyclist from Dad's hometown– both won gold medals.

Even Mum was excited because there was a woman, Raelene Boyle, who won track gold in the 400m. The spelling was different, but the name was the same as my Mum's.

***

Christmas was awesome for me. I DID get Star Wars, so much Star Wars, including an X-wing and the Taun Taun. I love the Taun Taun creature and you can even put Luke Skywalker inside its belly, like the movie.

Next year we aren't going to have Ms Masters. I will miss her songs, I tried really hard for her but she was always telling me to be quiet and to sit down. I didn't want a new teacher, though. Why do the teachers have to change? Of course, Mrs Swords was the best and would always be the best. I wonder if she still remembers me?

I call Evan sometimes but he hasn't visited yet and I think maybe he has new friends now. I have new friends, but it is sad how people forget other people like that. And it hurts too. Thinking about Mrs Swords and Evan forgetting me makes me sad. I don't forget anyone, even James Blundie, Peter and Amy from my first school.

I don't want anyone to forget me, it's not nice.

11

Chapter 11

The school year starts again, and our new teacher is Mrs Sharpe. She seems nicer than Ms Masters, but she seems ready for anything I try to do. And I soon learn that I have to be quieter and share better with others. I like her because she smiles. Not a Mrs Sword smile, but still a smile and she told me my drawing is getting better.

Just down the road from me is my new best friend, Nathan. My parents don't really like him so much, but I don't know why.

It is funny; we live opposite the school, but I am always late for class in the mornings (as is Nathan).

Still, it is good Nathan and I can play in the school after hours, even though we are not allowed. We ride our bikes in the school and do wheelies and jumps. I have inherited my sister's bike, which my Dad painted blue so it would look less like a girl's bike. Nathan has a BMX.

One day, we are without our bikes and we're just playing "war". This is where we pretend to be shooting each other and run and hide from each other. Of course, it is a lot more fun with more kids, but it is just the two of us.

We are heading home, maybe it is about 5 o'clock and we go pass our classrooms. We see the big double doors of the art classrooms open, which is strange.

So Nathan and I go in, calling out to anyone. One of these classrooms we use when we sing my favourite song 'Who stole the cookie from the cook-cookie jar'.

We open the door to the classroom, and there is paint everywhere! All over the floor, on the walls and so much mess. We know something has happened and so we both run home to my parents and tell them.

My parents call the police who come over and say someone had damaged the school. I don't understand at the time, but my parents later explain that the police thought Nathan and I had done it! My Dad is furious with the police.

The police leave and my parents say we won't help the police again. I never forgot that. I am also told to stay away from the school and to come straight home when school is finished.

I am already suspicious of the police, although I always liked their uniforms. A few months ago, I found a $2 note on the street. My parents told me that if I found money on the street, I need to take it to the police station. If after 3 months nobody has claimed it, then the money would be mine.

So I was very excited when I went to the Police Station 3 months later. But they said someone had claimed it. I don't know how I knew the policeman was lying, but I just did. I wanted that money for chocolates.

And now this! Stupid police! I have done the right thing, and they say I damaged the school.

For a while Nathan and I stay away from the school after class, but eventually we go back.

***

Shaerlyn awoke to their presence near. Farida, on the other side of the cave, stirred as well.

A group of the fallen, minds filled with madness, were approaching the entrance.

The fallen, the nephilim entrapped on Asgrax, normally wandered aimlessly. They, like most living things, needed oxygen. But there was no oxygen here now on this dark world.

Each day, each moment, they painfully died, yet cursed with immortality from their demonic parents, they lived on. Dying every moment of their lives compounded their misery and insanity.

They were always unorganized and Farida's voice had previously driven them far away. Now, however, they were back, driven by something.

"Don't listen to their minds," Shaerlyn cautioned Farida "There is only madness, pain and sin there."

Farida rose and sang a sweet melody that seemed to hang in the frozen air.

The fallen hesitated, their cries of pain increasing, but they continued marching on.

Something was wrong, something was very different.

Shaerlyn's sword appeared at her side, bursting to fiery life and illuminating her surrounds. The moaning and the cries grew louder as the fallen reached the cave entrance proper.

Farida sang on:

"Glory to the Almighty
    And the lamb that was slain
    That rose again."

The fallen, brutish giants of men all, shook under the power of her words.

Shaerlyn moved to the front. Apart from her voice and natural angelic strength, Farida was unarmed. She would have to protect her sister in this fight.

The first of the fallen came into the light, eyes a dull forest green. He wore nothing but a loincloth rag that did little to provide modesty. His feet were bare and huge as were his knuckled fists, clenched in agony and perhaps to fight.

He stood almost as tall as Shaerlyn, about the size of Goliath of old. Fortunately for young David, Goliath was mortal, but this beast was not.

The monster of a man stopped there, and his comrades hesitated behind him. Most of the nephilim had been especially intelligent once, but the few who remained were but a shadow of what they were long ago. They were still unbelievably strong, though.

Shaerlyn glanced back again, only to see Farida beside her and not behind her as planned. Shaerlyn swung her sword left and right, feeling its balance, and prepared for a charge.

The fallen had never acted this way before. Certainly when on Earth they had led mighty armies and struck fear into humanity, but now with minds of simpletons, how was it they were brimming to attack as a collective force?

Then she felt something else and knew who it was even before the laugh.

Behind the fallen were even more green eyes. Four demons and the imp, Hai Chen the Minotaur, barking at the fallen to move forward. Hai Chen even had his whip in hand, which he flung at the fallen's backs.

But it was the presence of the mighty seraphim Ki Koa that made her realize what this was.

The fallen were there to distract them and to mask the demons until the very last moment.

Ki Koa and his cohorts weren't coming for the soulgate, nor even young James beyond.

They were coming for her, for revenge.

***

Simon Smith was the apple of his mother's eye and could do no wrong. But wrong he did.

At the age of twelve, he had stolen cigarettes from his stepfather and from that day on he had stolen other things to keep up the habit. Even though he would be the legal age next year, there was no chance, with his acne, that he could pass for age if needed.

He actually hated his stepfather, not for any real reason, but simply because his mother spent so much time with him. Indeed, the stepfather was a jolly and pleasant man and tried to help Simon even with his homework.

Lately, Simon had got into drinking and had got himself invited to some parties. At one of these parties he had seen his friend have sex, and from then on it truly fascinated him. Again and again the image of his friend's girlfriend would replay in his head. Sometimes at night, in his dreams, she would come to him. She would do all kinds of things to him, things one could not imagine. Some were painful, some were strange, but she would finish with riding him to ecstasy. He would wake up sweaty and often with an obvious moisture in his pants. This would embarrass him, and he felt ashamed.

Every time he saw his friend, and his girlfriend, the image would replay.

The girlfriend would say "Hi Simon" and he would almost hear a hidden meaning in her words, like a small whisper in his brain. It would be "Hi Simon I want to sleep with you and drive you crazy. I want to feel you. Simon, it is you I want."

Of course she never said such things, but they seemed so real and he couldn't shake it. At night, EVERY night, she would come to him in his dreams.

A few days ago he had stolen a video from a video store. Luckily, he had the VHS format. He watched in fascination as two adults had sex and felt the stirring within. The first couple were okay, but the next couple, the girl had put her mouth down there. All he could think about was what that must feel like, and that night he was in luck that he dreamt of his friend's girlfriend doing that to him. He became obsessed with her and that sensation.

How could he know that the great demon, Gulya, succubus, had chosen him? That this was a favour and repayment to her demon colleague Ki Koa. Gulya, who had created so many of the nephilim herself, who had destroyed kingdoms through inciting lust, and relished the depravity of man, had chosen him- a weak, hateful young boy, as an instrument in a devilish plot.

***

The whole thing had been a trap and there was little Farida could do but fall beside her.

Quickly Shaerlyn went into action. She retreated with Farida to where the two cave entrance tunnels joined near the rock pools.

She was right, as two more demons appeared from the other way, in a bid to flank her and block her escape to the atmosphere of Asgrax.

They were trying to encircle them both.

She said to Farida "There is nothing you can do, get to the soulgate and get help. I will delay them as much as I can."

"But you will fall" replied a worried Farida, a look of horror on her sweet face.

"That may be my sister," Shaerlyn answered "But I will make it as difficult for them as possible."

"SHAER-LYN O SHAERLYN" a dark and mocking voice called out from the other end of the cave. Ki Koa. "I have a present for you."

"And I have a present for you!" Shaerlyn cried out and threw her sword, like a spear, through the ranks of the fallen.

In the thin air, it shot from her hand like a rocket. It slipped through three of the fallen and then cut off one of Ki Koa's ears; him being too slow to react.

The fallen wailed in pain, which seemed to shake the cave foundations. Shaerlyn grabbed Farida's shoulder and shoved her towards the soulgate.

"Go! Now!" She barked and watched Farida, eyes full of sorrow, turn and leave. It could very well be for Farida to protect the boy if she fell, but such a decision was not hers to make.

Shaerlyn watched Farida disappear. She had faced greater odds on Mars with Jael, and indeed in Hell itself, but the fallen were so impossibly strong and she was without aid.

She checked her armour then charged, smacking two of the Fallen down with her fists.

Hands wrapped around her to grab her, so many hands, but she ignited into a pillar of fire and emerged cherubim, four flapping wings beating away her enemies.

The fallen screamed once more, such a painful, horrible sound, and moved back from her Holy touch. Now the demons came to challenge her. She retrieved her sword.

***

Farida stepped through the soulgate to see James and Nathan heading to the schoolyard, after school hours. Something they were forbidden to do. She frowned.

Still, Shaerlyn was in trouble and she had to find some of her kinfolk to help. She took off and headed away as fast as she could.

Gulya stepped out from behind her vantage point and grinned. The demon watched the angel leave briskly, unaware of the succubus' presence.

***

Our local school was rather large. We normally played up the top, near my house, but since the police had accused us of doing some damage to the school, Nathan and I decided to play down near the chess club. There were some fields down there and a small grove of trees and flowers, where we sometimes played "war" and other games. It wasn't far from the dreaded handball courts, where each day we used to play the game of dodging tennis balls thrown at us. It was normally okay for most people, because you got to throw tennis balls back– but since I couldn't really throw a tennis ball well– I was an easy target.

We had been coming down here for a week and noticed nobody else. But today, near the grove, were three bikes. They were nice bikes too, and we hovered near them.

"Hey!" Said a voice, and Nathan and I spun. We were about to run, but then Nathan said it was okay. It was Simon who lived a few streets away, and Nathan had once tried a cigarette with him.

"What are you up to?" Simon asked in a friendly way. Two other boys appeared behind him, looking nervous.

"We are just playing" I said and everyone smiled and understood. I always enjoyed making new friends, and Simon was a LOT older than me.

Simon gestured us to follow him, and so we did.

***

The demons overpowered her and dragged her to the rock pool. All the while she could hear Ki Koa's laugh, mocking her struggle.

They shoved her head under the water, and her eyes grew wide with horror. Her face was looking through the soulgate, down to Earth millions of kilometres away.

She saw a boy with a knife. She saw baby James with tears in his eyes. What were they doing to him! She wrestled against the bonds that held her, but the demons were just too strong and many. She became a pillar of holy fire, but they smothered her in filth and transformed too. Only the imps and fallen, the nephilim, stepped back. They were much more vulnerable to holy fire, because they couldn't change to gases to avoid it or become a pillar of fire themselves.

She struggled on, closing her eyes to the scene on Earth, what they wanted her to see. One demon held her by her blonde hair, yanking on it painfully. Others kicked at her legs and back, weakening her and forcing her face farther into the rock pool.

She tried to concentrate. She opened her eyes and saw tears spilling down James' soft , freckled cheeks.

Anger filled her. Not this for young James! She could see Gulya, with a broad grin and flashing eyes, whispering into one boy's ear.

Farida was gone, safe, but young James' fate was too terrible to think about. Oh, how she had failed! How vain she was to think this was just about her, when the prized soul of a young human was worth so much more.

Her mind drifted under the pain, shame, humiliation and sense of utter failure.

She went back to another time, an aeon ago. A time when the beloved Israel was a myth, a hope. It was the time of Samson, of the tribe of Dan, a truly powerful man of the Great I AM.

He had slayed thousands of Philistines with his strength and was defeated, not in battle, but in the lure of flesh. The lust for a woman. A woman, herself, who had been corrupted by this very demon Gulya. The succubus who lay beyond the soulgate, next to a young boy, and near poor James.

Shaerlyn had watched the youthful Samson and admired his righteous anger when filled with the spirit of the Most High. He was not directly under Shaerlyn's care, but she watched his brave exploits. She was dismayed at his capture, this young Nazarite. The Nazarites were devoted to service and did not shave, nor did they cut their hair. The hair, and his vow, were Samson's strength. She thought about how they took his sight and imprisoned him. One moment of temptation had ruined him. She saw them cutting out his eyes, thought of the knife, and thought of the small knife in the boy's hands on Earth right now.

Yet, as she felt the strong clawed hands holding her, she saw the mighty victory that had come from Samson's disgrace. A disgrace she acutely felt now of herself. Samson was not beyond redemption, and neither was she.

With the last of his strength, Samson had prayed. Not to save his mortal body, but to be, again, an instrument of his celestial King. With all of his might, Samson brought down the Philistine temple, killing the ruling elite and becoming a hero once more, in his own death.

Through that whole terrible ordeal, HE had shown Samson a path to atone and make amends. The remorseful man took it with pleasure, becoming a beacon of hope for the future.

Shaerlyn's thoughts returned to the present. Asgrax. Her cave. But it was her cave no longer, spoiled by filth and corruption. This was no longer her sanctuary. She realized it was here she had hid herself, hid from responsibilities, from the pain. Until her patient King had summoned her back to the fight, only for her to be here, like this, now. Young James far away, young James about to lose his innocence. And she could do nothing.

They brought her up out of the pool for a moment of humiliation, Hai Chen punching her in the gut, Ki Koa smashing a fist into her face. She swayed. Then they thrust her head back again under the water as the pain rose like a scream through her body.

There was only one thing to do, ask for HIS infinite mercy. To be an instrument like Samson before her.

She felt more blows on her back, but it just numbed her. She gritted her teeth. Cried out to HIM. She cried out with all of her soul. Her hands found the edges of the rock pool and she grabbed hold of them. Her body shook.

The image of Samson stayed with her. His deeds. 'Let me sacrifice myself for the sake of this one child!'

"Thy will be done!" She roared like a lion. The water bubbled and frothed furiously and the sound escaped into the cavern.

The world of Asgrax awoke. Deep in its core there was movement once more. The surface buckled and tore, responding to her cry, as energy shot out from her.

"Shut her up!" Ki Koa yelled and yanked her face from the water. Fire spat from the angel's mouth, blasting into the cave, spraying all over Ki Koa's face.

Flames rocketed out of hands, her ears, her eyes, her nostrils and her wide mouth. The demons and others were engulfed in living, Holy flame, consuming all in sight. The demons fell back, wailing, Ki koa clutching the remains of his face. The fallen, the nephilim, evaporated instantly, becoming mere steam. The imps and demons retreated under the onslaught.

Enormous boulders crashed down and Shaerlyn knew no demonic hand held her now. The rock pool was but a shell, the water had all gone. But the soulgate remained.

She dived forward into the gate, as Asgrax rocked behind her, the cave collapsed in her wake, sealing all the creatures of evil within. Entombing them. The rock liquified and reformed as a layer of plasma, growing rigid and hardening in the cold planet's air.

12

Chapter 12

Simon led us through the school grounds. I had never played with kids this age before, and I was curious about what cool games we would play. I asked Simon if he liked Star Wars and he said he did, and I said that maybe we can play together one day. "Sure" he said. He told us he had found a cool place in the grove, a secret place. Actually, I had seen the area before. It was pretty cool, but close to the place some of us used as a toilet when it was too far to run back up to the school.

Nathan and one of the other boys were talking now, and Simon took me aside. He asked me to drop my shorts; I didn't understand any of this and I said I didn't want to but then he got angry and showed me his knife and said I should do it. I was terrified.

***

I grabbed my pants and pulled them up and ran. Nathan sprinted after me, shouting I couldn't tell his Mum that we would get in trouble.

I ran and ran. Simon and his friends had bicycles, but we only lived over the road from school. I ran up the hill, not knowing if they were chasing me or not. Nathan called after me and we changed directions towards his place. I still couldn't understand what had just happened.

***

Gulya spotted her, the demon leaping away from the boys in an instant. Shaerlyn's eyes did not cool, but glowed with the light of a thousand suns. She sealed the soulgate behind her, so no one from the cave could come this way, those strong enough to survive would be trapped. She could not hold it closed for long, perhaps an hour or two at James' age. Longer risked grave consequences for all. Something was different, too. She was weak, so utterly weak, as if it had bled everything from her. But her rage kept her going as she approached Gulya.

She saw James and Nathan fleeing. The pair had escaped somehow, but she saw one boy in pursuit get on a BMX bike, in a bid to cut James and Nathan off. Shaerlyn turned towards the boy and she began to pull out her sword. Suddenly she fell downwards , as a voice boomed from upon high. "Vengeance is mine." And she understood and turned again to apprehend the succubus.

Baby James had headed to Nathan's, running into the backyard before the boy on the BMX could reach them. Shaerlyn followed, but she knew she couldn't touch the sick minded boy on the bike. She would have to wait for her master to serve such justice.

As Gulya bounded into the backyard, Shaerlyn followed, but the angel knew she was in trouble. Her strength was fading fast. Nathan seemed as if he had forgotten the ordeal, was showing off to young James how he could throw darts in the air and catch them. Shaerlyn looked for Gulya. Where was she?

Gulya came around from the other side of the house and smacked hard into Shaerlyn. Shaerlyn fell over and slid along the ground, going through the fence, back into the front yard. Gulya pummeled her with six blows then leapt up. Shaerlyn reached for her sword, tempted to bring it into use but the hilt felt cold, no flame would erupt from it this day. All of Shaerlyn's powers were spent. As Nathan threw a dart into the air to catch with his hands, Gulya threw herself into the boy's German Shepherd. The dog reacted and bolted over, colliding with Nathan as the dart kept falling, right into Nathan's nose. Gulya laughed, but all that was heard was a dog's barking.

***

I watch fearfully as Nathan plays with the darts. I can't let myself think about what had happened at the school, that horrible, horrible school. I don't know how to explain it, but I know my parents would shout at me if they knew. I can't tell them. I feel bad.

Suddenly, I see the dog jump at Nathan, its dark eyes glowing green for just a moment. I watch, amazed, as the dart falls down on Nathan. Oh, Nathan! He screams, and in moments his mother appears. I see the dog fly backwards, like Nathan has kicked it away, but he can't have been that strong. His Mum wails and grabs at Nathan, telling me to go home. It scares me to go back on the street, but can't speak about it. I wet my pants and Nathan's mother notices.

"Oh James," she said, "Come inside quick and change. I need to take care of Nathan." I hurry inside.

***

The scene would have been bizarre to anyone who would have been watching. Shaerlyn dove inside the dog and found Gulya within, the poor animal going into a seizure as the two fought within her. The dog rolled around on the ground in great pain, and Shaerlyn knew they had to stop. She grabbed Gulya by the shoulders, throwing her out as she jumped out after her. Gulya scurried to her feet, but Shaerlyn reached out and snatched the demon's leg, causing her to fall again. Shaerlyn climbed on top of her and drew out her sword, dull and lifeless, metallic. Not even a whisper of a flame.

"It will have to do." Shaerlyn said as she smashed the butt of the old sword down on Gulya's teeth. The demon writhed, trying to grab the angel's face, reaching out to Shaerlyn's eyes hoping to gouge them out.

Bang!

Shaerlyn's blade smashed against Gulya's head.

Bang! Bang! Bang!

Gulya reeled under the blows.

Bang! Bang! Bang!

"Stupid demon!" Shaerlyn shouted.

Bang! Bang!

"When will this war end?"

Bang! Bang! Bang!

Gulya stopped fighting, her arms going limp.

Bang! Bang! Bang!

The sword slammed down, Shaerlyn did not tire.

Bang! Bang! Bang!

Poor baby James she thought.

Bang! Bang! Bang!

Poor Nathan, too.

Bang! Bang! Bang!

"Shaerlyn."

Bang! Bang!

"Shaerlyn!"

Bang! Bang!

Suddenly she felt a hand holding her, pulling her away.

Bang!

One more time. She looked up. Farida was there, Nephis too. Klaudos. Gabriel. Michael. Her family.

"Oh Farida," she cried and burst into tears. She drove the sword deep into Gulya's chest. It strained but eventually broke through the thick skin. Gulya didn't respond. The demon's eyes were shut. Michael came forward.

"Michael," she said, hugging him tightly. "Baby James," her voice trailed off.

"We know," he uttered, gesturing for Nephis to throw a chain around Gulya. "We know."

Uriel appeared among them and took Gulya away.

"You're exhausted," said Michael, steadying Shaerlyn.

"I AM strengthens me," Shaerlyn replied, but she knew she was sapped of energy.

Gabriel stepped forward, "We must hurry. The boy's soulgate must be opened soon. We were delayed because we went first to Asgrax. The cave is sealed, impossibly so. We know the fallen inside have perished and some of the imps. The demons of course live on but are entombed in heavy rock. So dense is it that they cannot even pass through it, nor can we. Perhaps similar to the planet Hell," his thoughts trailed off.

"Still," Michael cautioned, "if some are near the soulgate, they might find a way to escape once it is opened. For the rest, they will be on Asgrax for a long, long time. I am not even sure it is possible to dig out from there."

"Then the soulgate should remain closed," said Nephis. Many grunted in agreement.

"You know that isn't possible," sighed Shaerlyn, so glad to be amongst her kinfolk. "I need to open it, and soon!" Gabriel took her hand.

"You are not a Soulweaver Shaerlyn, but I can help you. We can drag or split the gate so its entrance is one place and its exit is somewhere else."

"But where?" Asked Michael.

Shaerlyn lit with understanding, "The Sun."

The angels clapped in agreement. Shaerlyn was fast, very fast, and the demons much slower. From the Sun's gravitational well, one could monitor most of the Solar System. Demons going through the soulgate could take more than eight minutes to reach Earth or to go to another soulgate. They would be exposed. Only a handful of soulgates sat on the Sun. They were important and were served by some of the strongest angelfolk.

"Okay," Gabriel said, "let us go."

Shaerlyn watched as three chariots pulled into the front yard.

"Ride with me," said Gabriel. Shaerlyn took his hand and smiled.

"Let us weave a soulgate in the Sun!"

***

When I got home, I told my parents about Nathan and the dog. I couldn't tell them about the boys in the school grounds because I was told not to play there and I would just get in more trouble. Still, I wanted to tell my mum, but I was ashamed.

They decided I shouldn't hang around with Nathan for a while, that Nathan was a silly boy. My Mum still called his Mum to see if Nathan was okay and he was. I still really didn't understand what had happened at the school. I remember what I had to do to get away, and I certainly had shocked and angered the older boys! I had been lucky in that I would never .... But still, all I really knew was that I would never go to that school after hours. My parents had been right. First the police saying I had done all of that damage to the art black and kindergarten. That was crazy! Worse; it was hurtful. I didn't really enjoy this school. Only Elizabeth and Belinda made me want to go there. Of course, there was Nathan, Warrick and Warren too, but that wasn't the same. Dominic and I had never been the same since he lost all his Star Wars toys in the sand, but that wasn't my fault either.

13

Chapter 13

Ah. The Sun. Shaerlyn floated in the orb of blazing light and heat. The noise was enormous as the fire burned and even matter consumed, deep in its core. Particles of antimatter were produced under incredible heat and pressure, annihilating the surrounding matter and producing a steady stream of gamma rays. Mind you, the Sun produced much less than many of its brothers and sisters.

Shaerlyn soaked in the heat. Glancing left and right, she saw the seven soulgates that were already there. The gateways to the Heavenly throne room. Until the time of the End of Days, they would remain here. Probably then, she thought, they would be moved to Earth. It was the privilege of the saints, also carried by Uriel, to depart from Earth this way. It certainly gave wonderful perspective. Uriel would take the hand of those who were worthy and they would ascend together, leaving Earth, farewelling love ones, farewelling the blue orb they knew as home, and through the fire of the Sun, enter the heavenly realm. Symbolically consecrated by fire, just as many had been consecrated by water on the Earth. Shaerlyn couldn't help but think about that very first day, especially floating here in the fire at the Sun.

In the beginning there was nothing, only the all present nature of the Creator. The angelfolk awoke, like they had been in a slumber, they had no recollection of their creation. And the Great I AM, the Creator, was there, He was indeed everywhere. Such joy Shaerlyn felt. Her first memories were of tears. Tears of happiness at seeing the beloved maker of all. All the angels wept. And on that day, they were to bear witness to how the world was made. The Great I AM never made the big bang; he was the very big bang and so much more. As every single point was made from the nothing. The nothing and the everything were in perfect harmony. Inside the everything, which perhaps didn't exist in more than an idea (yet Shaerlyn could see it somehow) the Spirit of the Most High drifted through the vapor and condensation. The Earth was carved out, everything was made, and yet there was nothing in the blackness. The entire universe was less in size, indeed had no discernable size, than an atom. And the Word was there, and HE gave Himself to all creation, the Word embodied in every particle that didn't yet exist; except it seemed in a collective imagination. Was it a mere vision, an illusion? Shaerlyn had asked herself at the time; and then when the Word was over all, the command was given;

"Let it be so!" In one instant, all was not an idea, or a particle, but no; all was then everywhere. And it was good and beautiful. The angels danced and sang. In that moment, the angelfolk touched each star and awaited the command.

"Let there be light!" And at that moment the suns were lit, and heat and warmth entered the void. It was explosive, exciting, and even the dark stars seemed to burn bright. Swirling clouds of gas and light swirled around. For Shaerlyn, the cannon fire at Waterloo was the closest thing to that sound. Angry explosions everywhere as the stubborn stars ignited in the order given. This Sun, where Shaerlyn floated, was one of the last to be lit. Shaerlyn had lit Betelgeuse, which aged an aeon before the Sun of the Earth was ignited. For the entire universe was beyond time. Yet the universe aged in that day. And the majesty of creation back then. And how creation was made in the image of its Creator. That was the sweetness of it all. What did the Creator look like? HIS spirit was everywhere, HIS Word held everything together, but the Father was the image of all creation. Creation; the perfect mirror. HE was the planets, moons, stars, the mountains, the rivers, the lakes, the trees. HE was the animals. Each of these things, before the fall, were not HIM but an image of HIM.

HE is a mountain, a river, a lion, a star; HE is all these things and more. Creation being just a copy of HIM and HIS nature, now an imperfect copy since the fall. And then the heavens began their motion, and time began. Soon after, all creation was finished. The crowning image of the Great I AM; man. The good. Before the heavenly war, before man's fall.

Shaerlyn remembered with pain the day of the heavenly war. After Michael had thrown Lucifer from the realm of Heaven himself, after Lucifer had fled with the army of fallen angels, Shaerlyn heard the doors of the great sanctuary open. The throne room was the home of the Great I AM, but the neighbouring sanctuary was the home of all creation. For within it lay the great scroll, written in the language that the Creator would one day give to his chosen people. This scroll was like no other. It floated off the floor and was curled around in an infinitely complex pattern. Circles of the scroll encased other circles like a giant spire of the galaxy it resembled, and indeed it was the great spire of the universe. Written upon it was all of creation, what was, is and would be. Written differently, no part of the universe would be the same. Shaerlyn was there, baby James was there, the Earth was there, and until that day, everything was perfect. Then the Word touched the scroll with HIS finger and a fire lit on one tiny portion of it, and Hell came into being. To this day that parchment burns a tiny fraction of the whole. This great scroll enabled Shaerlyn to fly, to draw her sword, to think. The words of the scroll allowed baby James to breathe, to play, to whine, to cry. The Sun did not shine without it. And it had been this scroll, perhaps more than anything else that Lucifer had coveted. Control over everything and all. It held the Nether, the Ethereal and all matter together. The world of spirit and the worlds of man. The soulgate was a merging, a window between these three realms. The scroll was a living document, and when a star died, when a soul left the world of man and when a soulgate was merged or split, the scroll was rewritten.

The mastery of it was maths more than any other science. Because it was indeed held together by such, and the mathematics of man, a mere shadow of it, a taste of it, the great drawer, the great mathematician, great draftsman, and indeed, the great musician. For music was one with the Word. Shaerlyn smiled at the complexity, yet simplicity of it all. That the Great I AM was staring each man, woman and child in the face. Every day belonged to HIM and had been written about or created by HIM. And now Shaerlyn was going to drag young James' soulgate here to the Sun. Gabriel was next to her and put his firm hand on her shoulder.

"Let it begin," Gabriel said, and he sang a sweet and soft melody. The Sun seemed to sing back and gave up itself the first essence of a soulgate, something to anchor the soulgate here. Shaerlyn chanted, a chant hidden in her being since times immemorial. She felt part of the soulgate begin its journey from Asgrax, carried on a mighty wind. Gabriel smiled, but his eyes narrowed. Singing on, he drew an image of a star; a star that contained all the words of the alphabet, the ancient alphabet of the angels, and drew out the commands in that sacred language. The letters appeared, as they did, an imprint at the base of the soulgate grew. Then, the soulgate appeared above them and the words of Gabriel lifted up to it, weaving into the fabric of the soulgate, the two becoming one. The soulgate was finished.

Shaerlyn nodded and thanked Gabriel. It was beautiful, shining red, on the outer edge the commands were written to hold it in place here, somewhat near the center of the Sun. Gabriel took Shaerlyn's hand, then cupped his other hand over the first. He whispered quietly; Shaerlyn felt the warmth flood through her like lightning. She reached for her sword with her other hand, drawing it out. The fire sprang to life, even brighter than the surrounding Sun. Gabriel pulled out a scimitar which also sprang to life. They grinned at each other;

"None pass the sword," said Shaerlyn.

Gabriel laughed and replied, "None pass the sword."

Shaerlyn commanded the soulgate to open. They braced themselves and waited to see who would exit. It was Hai Chen. Within moments, a clawed hand reached out of the soulgate. Shaerlyn recognized it at once as Hai Chen attempted to come through.

"Let us help", said Shaerlyn and Gabriel in unison and with their free hands grabbed the imp's arm, yanking him through. Hai Chen flew through the gate, Gabriel embraced him in a crushing show of strength and, as Shaerlyn let go, the two hurtled down and away, spinning end over end into the core of the Sun. Shaerlyn watched the archangel and imp battle from afar, from above. The two wrestled and struggled, Gabriel's' scimitar in his hand behind the imp's back, unable to be wielded. Hai Chen was a brute of an imp, the old Minotaur with the face of a bull. He was strong, very strong, but Gabriel, once being the Angel of Death himself, was no stranger to a fight. Gabriel transformed into a pillar of light, and Hai Chen wailed in his arms. He too transformed into two impossibly bright lights, both at the center of the Sun. She had never seen an imp with such power before, not even Cathor. Shaerlyn was almost transfixed, but she knew this had to end and dived to help her brother.

The Sun. The Sun. She could feel the warmth and glow. It was light; the warmth of HIM, but this didn't penetrate her spirit like being in the presence of the Great I AM. Being material now, with swords ablaze, the sun reacted to her presence, super-heated atoms becoming excited and exploding on her skin. Gabriel and Hai Chen too created a trail of light. It was beautiful to see. She arrived in time to see Gabriel trap Hai Chen's arms behind the imp's back. Hai Chen swore but could not best him.

"The chain," Shaerlyn called in relief. She pulled it out.

"Not yet," said Gabriel in stern concentration, "Reach around and grab his left arm. I want to show him not to fight the two fastest angels." There was a smile from Gabriel. Shaerlyn took the imp's enormous arm, using both of hers. When she had done so, Gabriel pulled out the other arm from behind the back and now Hai Chen hung between them, his body stretched.

Hai Chen, who she had once hunted in a maze alongside Raphael and the mortal Theseus. Hai Chen who had lured people to their deaths in the catacombs of Rome. Hai Chen who had tried to ambush her on Mars. Finally, in her reach.

"Shaerlyn," said Gabriel, "You are indeed fast, methinks you have been blessed with more speed as the aeons have gone by!"

Shaerlyn blushed. She knew she was indeed quick, but Gabriel was unquestionably faster and modest about it.

"I therefore challenge you Shaerlyn," the archangel went on. "I will take this arm and you the other. The first around the Sun, in a complete orbit, gets the Minotaur's head as a trophy!" Shaerlyn laughed.

"Okay," she said, and with that sped off to the left, Gabriel to the right and with ease, the arms of Hai Chen were ripped off. As they sped away, in their respective directions, they could hear the horrid screaming of the imp left behind. Shaerlyn skirted the sun at full speed, trailing Hai Chen's arm behind her. Faster and faster she went, space and time wobbling around her. The Sun flared in her trail. It was mere moments before she spied the wallowing form of Hai Chen, armless and useless. She reached out with her spare hand, her sword lit, ready to decapitate him. Her blade swung down, but there was no imp flesh. In a blink of an eye, Gabriel appeared, yanking the imp's body out of the way. Shaerlyn couldn't believe it. She had been so close. Gabriel laughed and held onto the snorting imp. Shaerlyn re-sheathed her sword.

Slowly, Gabriel reached his arm around the Minotaur's thick neck. Hai Chen gasped and fought, but Gabriel just tightened his hold. In one quick movement, he twisted the head and pulled it from its shoulders. The body sagged and drifted away. Gabriel held the head high. In the distance, other angels cheered from the soulgates they were guarding. Gabriel placed the head in his hands and eyed Shaerlyn;

"You tangled with this one more that most. Where do you want it?" Shaerlyn knew it was a temporary sport. Once they placed a golden chain on the body, everything would reform on the way to Hell.

"The Sun?" prompted Gabriel and gestured with his foot.

"Too easy," Shaerlyn said, grateful for this distraction Gabriel was providing. "Can you hit Mercury from here?"

Gabriel paused and calculated. Then he dropped the Minotaur's still sneering head on this foot and kicked. It spun off into the distance. Gabriel put his arm around Shaerlyn and they watched it fly off together. Shaerlyn pulled out her golden chain and nursed it. Words not spoken filled her head.

"You know what must be done next," Gabriel spoke from next to her. It was rhetorical of course; she knew, as Mercury welcomed its latest meteor strike. She knew, but inwardly she was holding it all back. Gabriel hugged his sister and took the chain from her; he snapped it around the leg of the headless and harmless Hai Chen.

"Who will guard the soulgate?" Asked Shaerlyn. She witnessed Hai Chen's head melt into a gaseous form and begin a horrid journey back towards them. She looked at her hands and felt the broken off arm disappear. Uriel had arrived.

"I will for now," Gabriel answered, "There is still a slim chance that another demon may come through. For now, we have had our sport. Time for you to grieve and heal."

***

Those words hung with her as she returned to the heavenly realm. Up past the giant waterfalls, landing on the edge where she could gaze over the stars, birth and destruction. Still, the presence of HIM lifted her and her tears that fell were those of joy, at least at this very moment. Her kinfolk cleansed her as she came in. She had been fighting hard for some eight Earth years, often against multiple foes. Fighting the prince of demons himself, through his traps and snares and watching helplessly as Jael disappeared, sacrificing himself. Watching baby James nearly die at birth and venture into risk many times since. Watching what befell the poor child at that school. Seen it all. They almost destroyed her so many times, she was so close to being one of them, the fallen angels, lost in battle. Now Le'dor roamed, creating chaos, after finally escaping from Phanuel. She could take comfort that Hai Chen and Gulya were imprisoned. That the imp Cathor shared their fate and Ki-Koa was seemingly entombed in rock so dense no claw or sword could penetrate it.

She looked over to the great lake where she had swum playfully for her Lord. She saw the great temple with the cloud of glory above it. She saw the saints meandering around. She recognized some. She wished more had made that decision. She walked past the bridge to the tree of knowledge, walked through gardens of bountiful fruit; of colours beyond imagination. In the distance, normally obscured by the temple in the foreground, stood the twin peaks of Sinai and Ararat, so named by the saints. They were not tall, but held in the belly between them, was the valley that she sought.

The valley of sorrows and the valley of lamentations; the valley of lamentations first and shallowest, before the valley of sorrows went off to the right and grew deeper. Here was the source of the river of life. The water that filled the river and lake came from here. Not from some precipitation, but from the tears of angels. The valley of sorrows was a special place to remember the history of the chosen people. The destruction of the temples, the years of captivity, the scattering of bones to the winds and the pain of the holocaust. The valley of lamentations was for the tragedy of all of man. There, in the valley, Shaerlyn stopped and got on her knees. She could not forget the horror of what had come to young James.

Shaerlyn wept. Her tears flowed, joining the river.

14

Chapter 14

Skipping with a rope was always very popular with the girls....sometimes a single rope or sometimes with an extra long one. I used to watch the girls skipping and hope to see their skirts fly up. The boys would giggle if they did. There was something so fascinating about women's skirts and why they dressed so differently to us, and that we could see their knickers sometimes.

But once a year was 'Skip rope for heart'. My sisters were quite good at it, especially Margaret, and now it was my turn. I was actually quite excited. I was already a mad runner and loved running everywhere, so I thought this would be fun to do. I had tried using Anne's hula-hoop the year before but I couldn't master that, but I thought skipping would be quite easy. How wrong I was, I was absolutely hopeless!

I could skip once or maybe twice, and then my feet would always come down on the rope. People said I jumped too high every time, and this was my problem, but every time that rope came down towards my legs I jumped up high to avoid it. I just couldn't do the stupid sport and it was sad because I wanted to. My sisters seemed like champions compared to me!

***

135

The one time of year I hated was cricket season. It meant an entire month of Test matches that went for 5 days. A game that went for 5 days? Usually at this time Dad was on annual holidays. And the cricket was on all day. My parents wouldn't even be watching it; they would fall asleep in their armchairs. But if I tried to sneak over and change the channel, they would wake up and say they were watching it.

TV was a world of wonder. There was 'Thunderbirds', 'Batfink', 'Mighty Mouse', 'Knightrider' with the cool 'Kit' car, 'the A- team', 'the goodies', 'the Muppet show', 'Monkey' and of course 'Doctor Who'. Last year they even stopped 'Doctor Who' for a time and replaced it with 'Monkey'. Dad was furious about this, but I also liked this other show. Now 'Doctor Who' was back on, with a different Doctor. And this Doctor liked cricket!

Our VHS had recorded 'A Bridge too far'- a fantastic war film. There were 'Convoy' with the cool trucks, 'Blazing Saddles' comedy and a few episodes of 'Fawlty towers.' We also had '9-5' with Dolly Parton and her big boobies.

My sister has been singing a song for the last year and it is a fun song. But I found it on the VHS, after 'Doctor Who' and the Daleks, after 'Blazing Saddles'. At the end of the videotape was the song.

I can't believe it, I am really in love. I mean I loved Mrs Swords; she was great. And I liked Belinda, and I think Elizabeth is my girlfriend.

This... is different.

I didn't even know the singer's name, but she was so, so pretty. And she was wearing scungies! Some called them bloomers. She was dressed in a cheerleader costume like you see on those American shows. And all the other dancers were wearing scungies under their skirts. But they were wearing black ones but this girl, this beautiful girl, was wearing red!

"Oh Mickey, you're so fine, you're so fine you blow my mind, hey Mickey!"

It was like she was wearing them for me, for me to see and she would jump and she would turn and I will see all of her scungies. I almost think that I shouldn't be watching, but why wouldn't she be wearing them for me? Where did she live? America? Could I live in America? I would live in America for her. I watched her every morning before school, turning the volume all the way down. I had to fast forward the tape every time and rewind it after I'd finished watching. Theresa could watch it with me.

When I go to school I look at the girls jumping and playing and I would see their scungies. Nathan, and sometimes Warrick and Warren, and I would discuss it and wonder what colour each girl was wearing. Most wore black, and I like black except my Mum and sisters would wear black when they played netball and that made me like black a little less.

I think I like blue best and then green, but we all got excited when we saw red. I don't know why. But for me, red reminded me of the Mickey song. One day, Belinda wore yellow, and we discussed it all day. No one could believe she wore yellow. Some of the other boys said we were making it up. All day, we tried to see and I think this made her uncomfortable and she stayed away from us but another boy told us that, yes; he saw she was wearing yellow too. We all decided that yellow wasn't our favourite colour, but it was still interesting that she had yellow because we hadn't seen them before.

I thought about telling Nathan and Warren about the video so we could watch it together, but what if the Mickey girl chose them over me? I decided to keep it a secret, even though the Vampire Club didn't keep secrets. They all knew I was a robot, a Dalek, and I was Superman.

***

There were two girls I liked at my school. Elizabeth and Belinda. Really, Elizabeth became my first girlfriend. Belinda always smelled strange, like roses. I started to think all women smelt like this, so it was a real shock when my mother farted once, as I thought only men did this. I certainly did not think their farts would smell like ours. My mother seemed embarrassed when she did this. Did she now know I knew the truth about women's farts?

I wondered a lot about girls. Many could do the splits, but I couldn't quite. I had gone to gymnastics with this boy for a while but we had had a fight so I stopped. But we never really did anything interesting, and we certainly never did the splits.

I had seen girl's private parts before in my life, and they were certainly strange. It was never something I tried to look at, it really didn't interest me but it helped me to understand why girls could do the splits and boys couldn't.

Girls have like a cut or a split that starts at the front called the vagina which goes all the way to the back at the bottom. So it is easy for their legs to split wide apart. Boys only have the split at the bottom, not all the way around. So it really isn't fair to expect us to do it too.

I would often go over to Elizabeth's house. We kissed in her bedroom once, and I liked that very much. I never got to kiss Belinda, ever.

Maybe it was strange, but I told Elizabeth that I liked scungies and she wore them for me without a skirt in the bedroom. She then showed me her mother's pair, and I tried them on. We danced around and laughed in them and had a lot of fun. Then there was a knock at the door.

Her mother came in and saw me in her pants and just said "Those are mine" and told me to take them off.

I quickly took them off and put my shorts back on.

I groaned and went home. I wondered if Elizabeth's mother would let me visit again–I felt very stupid being seen in her scungies.

***

Shaerlyn stepped into the room behind Kapyrol and watched as James' mother and father sat down in front of the teacher. It was parent-teacher night.

Mrs Sharpe began. "Thank you for coming. Mr and Mrs Campbell. I won't keep you long. About James, well. I was a little concerned when Ms Masters spoke to me at the start of the school year and cautioned me about him. That James likes to misbehave, that he rarely pays attention in class and daydreams. He also tries to be the centre of attention and sometimes gets in fights with other kids."

James' mother said, "But James liked Ms Masters, he was always telling us so. He just enjoys getting the teacher's attention."

"Yes, well. That's not the extent of it, I'm afraid. Some of James' behaviour hasn't been appropriate. A group of boys, including James, have been trying to look up the skirts of some of the female students. Other parents have complained, and we really think you need to talk to him about what is appropriate behaviour at school."

"He's just a boy." Dad said, "I'm sure he doesn't mean anything by it, I don't think it's sexual or anything like that, if that's what you're saying?"

"It doesn't matter what it is." Mrs Sharpe said, "It is not something that the school can tolerate and we need your help and James needs your help and for you to speak to him about it. He is also often late to class, which is not good. I will say, however, that I believe James has a lot of potential. In some areas he is slower than some of the other children, such as in art class. But he seems to grab information quickly and seems to be of a born leader. He just needs some direction both here and at home."

"Well, Jim and I will discuss it, won't we, Jim?"

"Yes, all right, we'll talk to him, certainly about the girls. It wasn't right that Ms Masters spoke to you about that.... he deserves the same chance as anybody else in a new school year and new teacher."

"Ms Masters was just concerned. I believe he has potential, as I said. James is a delight to teach, honestly, but he has some behavioural issues that need attention. Perhaps he needs to see somebody, I don't know."

"Thank you Mrs Sharpe, we appreciate everything you've done for James. We will speak to him." The mother said.

***

"Our son is a bit of a perv."

"Jim, that's a terrible thing to say– he just doesn't understand about these things."

"Well, he's not going to get girls that way. But I can't believe Ms Masters– that she just had to have a bit of a chat to Mrs Sharpe about him. That doesn't seem fair at all."

"No, it's not. I think we need to talk to James, together. I think Mrs Swords, at his last school,had the right idea. She said that if you tell him off, he is just going to sulk, get angry, upset or deny he did anything wrong. We need to come up with something else. I think I know something that might work. Just go with me on it."

"What about the program after school? You still want to do that?"

"He has problems with his coordination and this can affect his confidence, so I think he is overcompensating, making up stories and trying to be bigger and better than he is."

"Well, if he can improve his coordination he might do better with the other children." The father said, "What about swimming? You swim like a fish, but I'm a runner. I sink. James likes to run too."

"Yes, but a lot of children his age can already swim, so it's important that he learns too."

"Okay, hon, fair enough. Let's get him in here."

"Let's do it in his bedroom, come on."

The two walked to James's room and found him playing with his Lego on the floor.

"James, can you stop for a moment?" Said the mother.

James looked up and put down his Lego. "Yes, Mum."

"James, your Dad and I are here because... You're not in trouble or anything... But there are some kids at school, maybe some of them are your friends, making the girls at school uncomfortable by trying to look up there dresses and skirts and talking about their underwear. Now, I know you're our little Superman. And Superman is brave and strong and he protects other people around him doesn't?"

"Yes Mum." James said.

"Well, I need you to be our Superman at the school, okay? I need you to lead by example and make sure the other boys don't do this, okay? It makes the girls uncomfortable and Superman always tries to help people doesn't?"

James nodded.

"Superman wouldn't be doing things like this, would he?"

"Superman looked through Lois Lane's dress and saw her pink knickers." James said.

"Did he? In what movie?" Asked the Mum.

"The first one." The father chuckled for a bit. "I've got this. James, Lois Lane is an adult woman, not a child, and she asked him to do it. To see his powers. If she asked, it's okay. But only if it's an adult, not a child. And not for a young Superman either. When you get older, you will understand. But you are my son, we have the same name, and you want to be big and strong like Dad, don't you? You want people to respect you, and so you have to be a gentleman at all times. Now, can you make sure the boys at the school don't do this anymore?"

"Yes, Dad. I will stop those boys. I will protect the girls."

"Thanks James," the mother said. "Also, we have some exciting news. After school, you won't be coming straight home. There is a special class for you to help you with sports and things. Also, your dad and I decided, that you should learn to swim and we are going to organize some swimming lessons for you with an instructor. Then when we go to the beach, you'll be able to swim, won't that be great?"

"Yes, Mum. I want to swim like Aquaman, like in the cartoon. He helps Superman, you know?"

"Your Mum is an excellent swimmer, so maybe you will be an excellent swimmer too?" The father said.

"I would be so proud of you if you could swim, James." The mother said. She turned to her husband and then looked back at James. "All right, James. We will let you get back to your Lego. Just remember what we said about being Superman at school and protecting the girls, okay?"

The two men walked out, Smiling, the father said to the mother, as they reached the hall "Parents of the year, we are. I think that went well."

"He'll be fine. He just needs some help, with his coordination, learning to swim and how to correctly act around other people." Said the mother.

Shaerlyn looked on in silence. Wondering. She sat down next to James and watched him play.

Chapter 15

I didn't really understand why I had to go to this place after school several days a week. It was a strange place, like a large classroom full of various toys and games. They made me do puzzles and some of them were fun, most were quite boring. I really didn't like coming here, when I could have been playing with my friends.

There was a rope swing in the middle of the room and I loved to swing on that, but we mostly threw balls around, which was quite dull.

My parents told me how I had fallen on my head when I was very young, apparently falling out of a high chair, but I didn't remember that. They said that sometimes I misbehaved, but I didn't think I was naughty. They thought this place would help me.

To me, it was like a prison sentence, with no real reason to be here, but many times each week I was here doing silly puzzles and ball throwing. For what?

Later, my parents sent me to swimming lessons. I did not like the man at all. He was old and had a heated pool inside his house. I liked the shallow end, and I didn't even mind swimming from the deep end to the shallow end. But he would always make me try to swim to the deep end.

"Swim just to me" he would say and I would reach the spot where he had been. Yet he was further away. In the end my arms were flailing around, I was sucking in water, and it wasn't until I was nearly drowning that he would help me.

It was a terrible way to learn, and it inspired no confidence in me, and to look upon the inky blackness of the deep end scared the hell out of me.

From then, I was afraid of deep water, which was made so much worse when the movie 'Jaws' came out. The idea of my feet dangling down in the sea became something of my nightmares, and I often dreamt of it and drowning.

***

I had a new best friend, Warren, who I always got mixed up with Warrick. Nathan and I saw little of each other since that day with the older boys. We never played together after school anymore. Nathan had also taught me a bad word, and Mum washed my mouth out with soap. This made me angry with Nathan, too.

Warren and I would ride along the bike path near his home...it seemed to go forever. There were underpasses for the bicycles too, so you could ride under the roads. We would ride as far as Jameson shopping centre.

I loved Jameson shopping centre, and especially the water park next to it. In summer we would go down the slides all day. The first time I got sunburnt there too, oh it hurt so much!

One day, Warren and I were riding, and he stopped at one of the underpasses. The road traffic we could hear above us, but no one could see us down here. From out of his pocket. he pulled some matches. We lit a fire there and watched it burn. It was cool. We both started to leave, but then I remember to get the box of matches he left behind. Warren was already a few hundred metres away by this stage.

I grabbed the matches and then started to ride away. Behind me were voices, and I saw some children coming down from the road. Suddenly I noticed a policeman with them. As I turned to focus on riding away as fast as I can, I heard the policeman call out for me to stop. I ignored him and stood up on my pedals to sprint; I was terrified. I had started a fire, but it had only just happened...how could the police know about it so quickly!

I had had some problems with my bike pedals, namely they often fell off–mostly the left one. No idea why. True to form, when I needed them the most, my left pedal came off, and I crashed my bike. I got up quickly and tried to put it on again to ride away– but the policeman was right there and there was nothing I could do. Would I go to jail?

The policeman asked me for my name and asked me what I was doing and if I had started the fire. I said I didn't, some other boys did, but he didn't believe me. He told me the police station was only 100 metres away from the underpass and that the other children had smelt smoke and done the right thing and come to the station. He got my address and told me he was going to speak to my parents. I was so ashamed. Warren was nowhere to be seen.

When I got home I was worried I would be in a lot of trouble, but my parents said nothing. Did the police call them?

Just a few weeks later there was a big fire at Jameson shopping centre. I always wondered how it started. Was it Warren or some other boys who lit a little fire like mine...or was it something else? I was sad that my favourite shopping centre was closed, though.

***

That night was my first dream of the eye.

I was in the suburbs of Cook, over where Warren lived, one suburb over from Macquarie. I recognized the ever many cul-de-sacs behind his home. I was in a sea of houses, like some giant maze. I felt familiarity with some of the streets and then, in a fleeting instant, the eye was gone.

I wandered and wandered with little aim, but it seemed there was some pressing need. I didn't know what I was looking for, but I knew I was looking.

Then I turned the corner into one cul-de-sac and there it was. I think there she was.

The eye.

The eye was on some plant like base, with the eye roaming on some giant stalk that could stretch out of it.

The eye seemed comforting, almost motherly, and I remained with it for a while. But when I went to leave I also felt something else, obsession. It followed me, stretching longer and longer.

I broke into a run, but the eye seemed to almost keep pace, following me by stretching its long neck, as we went from street to street.

Finally, I lost it and woke up. It seemed so real.

I dreamt of it many nights after this and I am sure I would remember this dream for a long, long time. Sometimes I would search for the eye, but once I found it I did not know if I was to love or fear it.

I did not know what the dream meant, why I would remember it or the actual intentions of the eye within it.

***

It was a surprise, but I knew where we were going, where I had always wanted to go— Black Mountain. We are driving up the road just now; it twists and turns so much and always up, up and up. I can see Canberra through the trees and it is very far below us. What if we make a mistake and fall off the edge? Wow, it is so steep!

Black mountain can be seen from all around, it has a huge television station up there or something. Some sort of communications tower. I have seen it on postcards, but never in person. It is just so high. I wish I could live up there. It is like something from Empire Strikes back or some other film. It is very impressive (new word for the day; I am trying to use it as much as possible.)

So now we are at the top, in the carpark and my Dad just told me we can go inside. I am so going to do that and I run ahead, even though my Mum calls me to slow down and wait for everybody else. You can see everything from up here!

***

After Black Mountain, my parents sat me down with my brother and two sisters.

My sisters were arguing again, I did not know about what. But Mum told them to be quiet. Both gave sullen looks, like they were both about to win the argument.

Dad looked like he was about to say something, but my mother smiled and gestured she would do it.

"We are moving to England." She said.

My sisters looked at one another and began jumping for joy and clapping. I looked at my brother, confused. His expression was blank, his eyes glancing at the food still on the table.

"When?" Asked Margaret excitedly, jumping up and down like a jack-in-the-box. I smiled at the thought.

"Yes, when?" Asked Anne, who was probably slightly less excited than her sister, but then she was the eldest and (as she used to say) the 'Most mature'.

Mum said, "We will arrive just before Christmas," She paused "We will have Christmas in England."

"Snow!" My sisters yelled. Now THAT was cool. Every Christmas we had a family barbeque, Christmas was always hot. Afterwards I would watch cartoons at home about Santa, Frosty the Snowman and snow, snow, snow.

"What about Father Christmas?" I asked, "How will he find us in England?"

Mum smiled sweetly then gave a serious look "We have written to Father Christmas already, and he knows where we will be. His reindeers are very clever and they know how to find us."

"Rudolph can probably smell your socks" Margaret suggested, I think she was trying to insult me, but I didn't quite understand how. My socks didn't smell, did

they? Besides, when Margaret came back from athletics, she stunk like a Pepe Le Pew.

Anyway, I was happier now that I knew Santa knew where we would be. I would not say I have been a good boy this year, lighting that fire and doing other things, but maybe Father Christmas didn't know about these things? I had been a better boy than last year; I protected the girls even if it meant fights. And last year I got lots of presents.

I started thinking about the snow. I had only seen it twice. Once it snowed here in Canberra, for just one day. But it wasn't even enough to make a snowman or have a real snowball fight. The other time was when we went to the Snowy Mountains, which weren't that far from Canberra. We were supposed to see the snow, but many roads were blocked and we got sort of lost. So I only saw it on the sides of the road.

I remember the trip because, when we got lost, we stopped at a pub on the way back down. There was a man there who had a baby kangaroo, a joey, and I got to hold it. It was so cute, covered in grey fur. I wanted one just like it and my Dad told me he had a small kangaroo once, when he was young on a farm.

I wanted to have one then as a pet, my parents said maybe, but Margaret said people weren't allowed to have pet kangaroos. She was always spoiling things, thinking she knew everything. Besides, that man at the pub had had one.

But England...I didn't really understand what this all meant. I had heard about it from school, but I would even have trouble finding it on a map.

I thought about my life here in Canberra. Warrick, Warren, and Nathan. Belinda Campbell and Elizabeth. I mean, I always felt Elizabeth would be my girlfriend forever. Okay, I didn't see her after school anymore because I had those stupid swimming and 'throwing the ball for no reason' classes.

I thought again about starting that fire, getting in trouble with the police for it, and also them saying that I damaged the school. My parents wouldn't be happy if I ever said it, but the police made me angry. I hated how they had said I had vandalized the school, when I hadn't, plus when I handed in that money and I never got it back. I was afraid of them, though. I don't think they told my parents about the fire, because my parents would have said something. But I was always nervous about it and ashamed.

One thing that was cool about Canberra, was that so many people knew I was Superman....I was worried that in a new place, people wouldn't believe me.

Another memory lingered, a dark memory of even greater shame and confusion. I felt one day I would meet those boys again, who had made me do those awful things. I heard that one of them, Nathan had told me his name was Simon, had been hit by a truck and broke his leg and was walking with crutches. I don't know if I had prayed something would happen to him (I felt guilty that maybe I had wished this), but I was still afraid of him and the others. Especially with that knife.

Still....Canberra was home. There was the totally cool war museum, which had a Lancaster bomber, and I just loved this huge plane. There was Black Mountain tower, which I also loved and finally been up to. And Canberra was full of crazy roundabouts, which my Dad often drove too fast around and that was fun, even though my Mum didn't like it when he did it.

"Do we have to go?" I asked.

My Mum fixed her eyes on me, her face ever smiling "Of course we do James. Your Dad is going to do a very important job there. He is going to be the Navy Rugby coach."

"What about all my toys?"

"They will come by ship, James. We can't take everything on the plane. And you

will have new toys at Christmas while we wait for them."

"But I love my toys," I said glumly.

I could feel the excitement from my sisters, but it did not impress me.

16

Chapter 16

Stupid Dominic! He was talking about girls in a bad way at recess and I told him to stop, like Superman would. Then he went around telling people I wasn't Superman and that I had stolen his toys. This got me angry, and I pushed him.

Ms Masters was on playground duty and grabbed me by the ear to the Principal's office. I begged, and the Principal agreed to not call Mum this time. He let me go to return to class.

When I got to class, they were reading the 'Magic far away tree.' And there was a story about Jane Slap who would hit young children.

Dominic then started saying I was 'James Slap' and everyone laughed. So, at lunch, I took off my school jumper, wrapped it around and whipped him with it.

Other students took off their school jumpers and were hitting each other. Mrs Sharpe arrived this time and looked straight at me and escorted me back to the Principal.

Mum came to school, and they sent me home with her. When I got there, I wasn't allowed to watch TV or play with my toys but wait for Dad to come home.

Dad had hit me once with the belt, he tells me, when I was much younger but I don't remember this. This time he used the Fly Swat, and it stung so much. All I was trying to do was protect the girls, and this is what happens! Life is so unfair, even when you try to do the right thing. I did what they told me to. And they wouldn't listen to me, said I was making excuses.

***

I might be a morning person, but I was asleep when Dad came rushing into the room, shaking me awake, and picking me up in my pyjamas and running with me to the lounge room.

I had absolutely no idea what was going on. My sisters were on the lounge suite yawning and Mum followed us in carrying Stuart.

The TV was on and I could see... boats?

Dad took centre stage next to the TV and said, "This is the America's Cup. It is a yacht race that has a trophy that America has kept for over 100 years. No one has beaten them in all that time. But if we win this race, Australia will get the trophy."

I don't see how this has anything to do with us. Athletics or the Olympics I understand. Even rugby. But this?

"Just watch, just watch. You will remember this moment forever."

"Do we have to?" Asked Margaret.

"Yes, do we have to?" Asked the yawning Anne.

"Anyone like a cup of tea?" Asked Mum.

Stuart climbed off the lounge suite and moved closer to the TV and sat down. I shrugged and in a moment joined him.

Dad explained that there was this man Dennis Conner, and he was a fantastic sailor. And he was leading the American team. Australia's boat was led by a man called John Bertrand, but Australia had a secret weapon. There was this special invention by this man Ben Lexcen, the winged keel. Dad explained it gave better lift on the boat when it was on its side, which increased the waterline length. The keel at the bottom of the boat moved as well. This allowed maximum speed and stability.

The race started slowly and as we watched it unfold, the Australian team went out on a different course, much further out and it seemed Americans were going to win.

"They're going out wide to get better air, though they will go faster they will need to cover more ground. It was a tactic I used to do when I was racing yachts in the Navy." Dad said.

I didn't know that Dad raced yachts, of course I knew he was in the Navy. I knew about orienteering, athletics and rugby but now sailing too?

As the race wore on, the Australian team caught the Americans and they seem to fight it out, going side to side and not in a straight line. Dad called this tacking. I have no idea, but they seem to be working very hard.

And suddenly Australia was in front and my Dad was screaming at the TV, even my sisters were clapping and cheering and I began too. I couldn't help it, it was becoming exciting. Could we win?

And then it happened as the yacht Australia II raced ahead and won. Our entire family went nuts jumping up and down, shouting and dancing. I could even hear the neighbours doing the same. I think the whole street, maybe the whole country, this was unbelievable.

***

"Interesting" said Kapyrol, standing behind the lounge suite.

"I admit, I don't get it," said Shaerlyn.

"I thought I was the only one," said Farida "So this is….a sport?"

"Apparently," Kapyrol said, "Maybe trying to create famous battles. I was at Trafalgar, with giant ships blasting away with cannons, trying to outmaneuver each other…"

Shaerlyn nodded "I was at the great sea battle between Rome and Egypt, the folly of Marc Anthony and Cleopatra. No cannons back then. Arrows and ramming and leaping to the other ship and fighting hand to hand."

"Yes, well, I was at none of them." Farida said, "Look how they're celebrating. they weren't so enthused at first, but by the end of the…race I guess you would call it…they were all united and excited for the outcome."

"The twins here? Phanuel?"

"We're here," said Haniel "Phanuel has been recalled to fight Le'dor. You haven't heard?"

"No, I have not. I heard some news they fought in the cosmos, but Le'dor escaped. That's it." Shaerlyn said, "Ever since I lost Jael, we lost Jael…I…well my focus has been here with James."

Netzach put a hand on her shoulder, then Farida and Kapyrol did the same "We are all here for you sister and you still have us. We just need to keep faith and stay true to the mission."

"I just don't want to face him battle if he has fallen."

"We know." Farida said, "Look, James is going back to bed. let's return to Asgrax and I will sing you a hymn."

"A good idea" Kapyrol said "I will be here or nearby."

"As will we" Haniel and Netzach said in unison and the two faded from Shaerlyn's sight.

***

Well, here I am. I must admit being on a plane is very exciting. It is huge! We are flying by QANTAS and one stewardess told me we could meet the captain and go to the cockpit with Stuart once we have taken off. Cool. I think I would love to be a pilot, of course a fighter pilot would be better or pilot a rebel X-wing. Dad isn't keen on me being an 'airy fairy' in the Air Force, but the Navy is supposed to get a new aircraft carrier from England and call it H.M.A.S Australia. Maybe I can fly from that. My uncle was an airy fairy, a musician in the Air Force, and Dad said there was no way I was going to ever join " A bunch of girls." Not quite sure what that meant, but I don't want to be a girl.

The stewardess gives a speech about safety and I pay close attention, reading all the emergency procedures. This is important to know. I then feel the plane moving forward and Dad explains we are moving onto the runway.

Then suddenly, I can hear a roaring noise and we gather speed. I try to look out the window but my sister, Margaret of course, is hogging it. The plane is getting faster and faster. I feel my stomach lift and it isn't exactly pleasant. Almost like I am about to be sick. My seatbelt is fastened, but I am still nervous.

This is my second time on a plane, the first was an airy fairy, I mean Air Force, Hercules transport plane. When we moved to Canberra, we used that. That plane was much, much noisier, and you had to wear earplugs. You also had to sit in funny seats made of webbing.

So now I am in the air and I smile and my younger brother, who I can see also thought it was pretty cool. Our first stop would be Singapore, said Mum, and there would be lots of good shopping there.

I missed my toys. I could only bring a dozen of my Star Wars figures. I had a stormtrooper, rebel pilot (Like maybe I would be), Darth Vader, Chewbacca and also a few bounty hunters. I didn't have Boba Fett, though. He was my favourite, but I haven't been able to buy him yet, there were none at Jameson shopping Centre.

My favourite that I already own, which I took on the flight with me, was the Taun Taun. This was a friendly animal that Luke and Han had ridden on.

But what I am going to miss most of all was Theresa. I still can't believe we aren't taking her. She is my cat! Dad said she couldn't come because she would have to spend months in Quarantine and it wouldn't be fair, but being without me isn't fair either. We gave her to my Aunt Glenda to look after, but I want her back when we come back to Australia. I don't know how long it would be, Dad said two years, but I know Theresa wouldn't forget me. We also gave our car to My Aunt Keitha. I was sad about this too, but Dad said we would get another in England. Why do we have to always give away things? The boat, my motorbike, the car and Theresa. I was sick of it.

The plane has been in the air for about an hour, when I got the strangest feeling that someone was watching me. I glance over to Margaret on my left. Ha! She was already asleep. I look to the right but the aisle seat was empty and the row over was full of boring old people, reading.

I play again with the Taun Taun and the feeling returns. This time I don't look up but pretend to continue playing. A weird feeling comes over me, a peace. My eyes become heavy and I close them. In my dream I am still on the plane, Margaret isn't next to me now, but there is someone on my right. I slowly turn.

Next to me is a beautiful woman, with long blonde hair and green eyes. Her eyes are so green they could have been lightsabres. She smiles at me when I look at her and I see a slim, soft hand reach out and rest on mine.

I feel everything is going to be okay. Blushing red, I smile back and open my mouth to say something. Somehow I know this woman.

Then, there is a sudden shaking, and my shoulder hurt. It wakes me up. My brother, Stuart, has just punched me!

"Hey!" I said, trying to stand up, but the seatbelt held me.

"James, James," Stuart said "The stewardess says we can go to the cockpit!"

I quickly throw off my seatbelt and head after him to the front of the plane.

Half way there, I turn and stop –half expecting the beautiful woman to be there. She isn't, but the memory of those green eyes lingers.

***

Shaerlyn smiled as she watched the boys run forward to the cockpit. Their time in Australia was at an end.

Now young James was heading overseas. His life had already been full, but Shaerlyn knew the journey and adventure had just begun.

***

In the dark place, Jael screamed.

About the Author

Author of 4 novels and 1 book of poetry, Yaakov has been writing since the age of 12. Now living in the Republic of Georgia, he is accused of being an Australian.

You can connect with me on:

https://www.facebook.com/YaakovCLuiHyden

www.ingramcontent.com/pod-product-compliance
Lightning Source LLC
Chambersburg PA
CBHW061530120726
48001CB00004B/1472